Order of the Dragon

Siobhan Muir

DEDICATION

Dedicated to all the women and men who thought Dracula didn't get a fair shake.

ACKNOWLEDGMENTS

Writing a book is never really a one person job, and writing a series is especially difficult alone. Keeping track of details is so much easier when you have help. Not only does it take a great deal of hard work, editing, and research on the part of the author to get things correct, but without my compatriots, there'd be a lot more mistakes. Great thanks go to Silver James who made sure the typo bugs weren't too big and the story made sense from start to finish. Thanks to Kris Norris for designing the most glorious new cover art.

CHAPTER ONE

Aliandra locked the clinic doors behind her and stepped out onto the wet and windy sidewalk. She sniffed the air, shoving her gloved hands into her down jacket's deep pockets. Snow wasn't far off, the northern wind heavily laden with moisture as it pushed against her chest. While the climate wasn't that different from her home in Peru, she still preferred warmer temperatures.

Then why, in the name of the Goddess, did you move to the Warbler Peninsula in northern Michigan?

Aliandra sighed at the contrariness and huddled down into her coat as she strode toward home. She'd been drawn to Three Lakes by the very powerful presence of a *Morukai* woman and the other Elder Races almost a decade earlier. The call of the *Morukai,* an ancient Shamanic race speaking for the Goddess, extended to all the Elder Races. They came to protect such a speaker, namely Kate Blackamber, and Aliandra bet her tail barb it was the reason she'd settled here.

But the Morukai *isn't the only reason I came to Three Lakes.*

Aliandra increased her speed, trying to outrun the truth. But the certainty trailed after her, laughing in the sounds of the last wet leaves of autumn scraping over the sidewalk in the wind.

He lived here in Three Lakes.

"Pah!"

She snarled as she damn near ran down the sidewalk to her little house. She had her keys out and ready as she raced up the porch steps and crashed into the door. Her hands shook, but she forced the key into the locks and thrust the door open, slamming it behind her to shove away the truth.

Dark, cold, silence met her and she leaned against her door, trying to calm her breathing and her heart.

Dr. Keener would tell you to take a Valium. She snorted, her humor slowly returning. *Not that it would help or affect a Wind Runner at all. Which just means I'm fucked six ways from breakfast.*

Shaking her head, she pushed herself off the door and switched on the lamps in her living room. Light flooded through the small space filled with brightly colored rugs and cozy plush furniture. She passed her small antique writing desk in her hurry to get to the brick fireplace, crouching on the hardwood floor to pile wood behind the grill. She stacked the wood in a harmonious pattern taught to her by a Hopi medicine man, muttered a prayer of gratitude to the Goddess, and spat at the heap. Bright, hot flame engulfed the kindling and a wash of heat spread over her and into the house.

Aliandra sighed with pleasure, reveling in the fire's greeting.

She would've sat there all evening if her phone hadn't chirped at her with a message announcement, rousing her from the fire's allure. Aliandra groaned, sweeping her hand through the fire in farewell, then rose to retrieve her phone from her purse.

Sliding her finger over the smooth screen, she grimaced when she saw the text message on her "emergency line". But her blood ran cold when she read the message.

Injury at the Library. Archivist has fallen. Please come immediately!

Oh hellfire, why did it have to be me on call tonight?

Aliandra waved at the fireplace, focusing on the moving currents of air in her home, and snuffed the beautiful flames in one motion. She hoped the Fire Spirits would forgive her abrupt actions as she stuffed her phone in her purse, grabbed her keys, and shot out the door into the frigid evening once more.

****

Drake MacGregor cursed his clumsiness and his distracted state as he leaned back against the stacks of books in the little Three Lakes Library Archives. If he hadn't been so distracted he would have fed yesterday or the day before, eliminating the need for any help at all. But since Kate Blackamber's wedding, his concentration was shot to hell, and now he didn't have the energy to heal quickly or without help.

Good excuse, but that was two months ago.

Bailey, his sweet and flirty assistant, had called the doctor on call at the Three Lakes Clinic despite his protestations. She'd insisted and now he was stuck waiting with his foot elevated while Bailey kept the people in the library occupied. Dr. Paul Keener would laugh at him and tell him to take it easy at his age, then give him a brace and send him home. It would be fine as long as Paul showed up.

Dear Goddess, please send Dr. Keener.

Drake tried to ignore the plaintiveness of his inner voice, but the thought of seeing the other doctor, the alluring, exotic woman who smelled like mesquite campfires and spicy chocolate, sent his head into a spin. She'd been at Kate's wedding, flashing her seductive smile at him as she gazed into his very soul with peacock-green eyes. His hands had itched to trail down her thick, glossy braid of black hair, holding fast to it while his mouth swooped into to plunder hers.

This is why I'm such a mess.

It had taken every bit of his considerable control to remain cordial and gracious when his mind filled with images of sinking his fangs and his cock into her warm body. Dr. Cantora del Viento electrified him like no other woman had since his dear Ilona, and he didn't like it.

He had no business thinking about anyone in that fashion. Family ties were fine. Drake had been glad to see his nephew Fredrick MacGregor with his wife Bridget, the Avatar of the Goddess, at the wedding, but even the Avatar had been eclipsed by the erotic and exotic doctor.

"Oh, thank goodness you're here!" Bailey's voice reached him all the way in the Archives. "He's in the Archives room and I think he's broken his leg."

Drake grimaced. He could see Paul chuckling and shaking his head, and he expected the refined man to tsk over him with a look of resigned humor. But the vision that stepped through the doors of the Archives behind Bailey stopped his heart and stole his breath.

Dear Goddess of all, she's here.

Dr. Aliandra Cantora del Viento looked flushed and windblown, tiny wisps of hair escaping from her braid under her hat. It must have started snowing because her shoulders showed water spots from the melt. Drake's groin tightened as the lights caught in her unusual colored eyes, beautiful eyes he wanted dive into and rest forever.

Bloody hell, I'm too old, too broken, and too cursed for her.

Grateful he wore loose slacks to cover his hardening erection, he tried to reposition himself as she surveyed the room, taking in the toppled bookshelf and scattered books in disarray around him. He'd been weak and distracted and clumsy, not a common combination for a vampire, and now he paid for his neglect.

"Trying some extra acrobatics, Mr. MacGregor?" Dr. Cantora crouched beside him.

Her sultry voice hardened him even more and he could barely grunt in acknowledgement of her remark, losing his manners completely. Her spicy scent flooded over him and his canines elongated in his mouth, itching to sink into her delicious flesh. She gave him an amused smile as examined his elevated foot.

"May I push your pants up to examine your leg?"

She could push his pants all the way off and he'd cheer her on, or at least his cock would. But Drake tightened his lips over his fangs and nodded stiffly.

Dr. Cantora lost her smile to concentration as she gently grasped his foot and pushed aside his clothes. Her hands burned hot against his chilled skin and the urge to crawl into her lap and wrap himself around her made him groan. Drake jerked as he aborted the motion and she froze, mistaking his movement for pain.

He felt pain, just not in his leg. *Why didn't I wear boxer shorts today?*

"Did that hurt?"

"No, ma'am, just surprised me, that's all."

She inhaled slowly as her hands returned to his foot and he tried to think of entering all the books still listed in the old card catalog to keep from bursting his zipper.

"Will he be all right?" Bailey asked, making him jump again. He'd forgotten she remained in the room.

"I believe so." Dr. Cantora lightly massaged his leg up closer to the knee and he hissed in pain. Perhaps he had broken it after all. "It feels like a fracture rather than anything more serious. I think we can get away with a stabilizing brace and light cast, but we'll have to get you to the clinic for X-rays."

No, no, no! He couldn't be alone with her at the clinic

after hours. He was too hungry and too unsettled. He'd attack her and he swore he'd never do that to a human again. Drake shook his head and opened his mouth to protest.

"No arguments, Mr. MacGregor." Dr. Cantora held up her hand before he could say anything. "You need to have it X-rayed and bound. You can't even walk. You're leg is badly swollen already and you could do irreparable damage if you walk on it. I have a wheelchair in my car and we'll get you to the clinic without a problem."

She rose fluidly and his mouth watered while his mind traipsed to places it shouldn't. If she was so lithe in day-to-day life, how would she be writhing under him?

Bloody hell.

She looked over her shoulder at him, cocking her head at a thoughtful angle. Her eyes glowed iridescent green for just a moment in the library's lights and a small smile quirked the corner of her sensual mouth. Drake growled under his breath as he sat up and rested his hands in his lap, covering his obvious arousal.

Please leave so I can recover what little dignity I have.

As if she heard his plea, Dr. Cantora ducked out of the Archives, taking her heat and delicious scent with her.

Drake missed it immediately. *Dammit.*

"Oh, Mr. MacGregor, I'm so sorry this happened." Bailey wrung her hands, concern suffusing her face. "I should have been in here helping you."

"No, no, Bailey, you needed to be out front." He waved her off, hoping she wouldn't notice he slurred from hunger. "I'm just clumsy, that's all."

Bailey frowned. "What were you doing to fall so badly? You should've asked for help. I was just reading."

He wanted to smile at her attempt to hide her worry by scolding, but her warm, coppery blood scent called to him and he had a hard time reining in his hunger. He leaned toward her before he could stop himself, and she threw herself into his arms, hugging him tightly.

"I'm so sorry this happened to you. I wish I could make it better."

Oh, you can, my dear. Just let me sip from your fountain of life and you'll help me...

Drake caught himself before he'd done more than nuzzle her throat. His lips rested against the pulsing vein under her skin. All he had to do was open his mouth and take just a little.

No, no, I can't. It wouldn't be right. But an insidious thought reminded him it would save him from feasting on Dr. Cantora when she took him to the clinic tonight and his resolve wavered as his arms closed around Bailey's back.

A hiss of surprise and dismay pulled him back from his lustful trance to meet the burning gaze of Dr. Cantora. She stood in the doorway behind the wheelchair, her expression a perfect mask of professional disinterest, but her eyes churned with an emotion he didn't have the clarity to decipher.

Drake immediately released Bailey, jerking back to slam into the pile of books behind him. Bailey squeaked as the books cascaded around them, adding more jumble to the already destroyed room.

"Oh, God, I'm sorry. I didn't mean to hurt you." Bailey stood up. "I'm so glad Dr. Cantora is here to take you to the clinic. Call me when you're done so I know you're okay. Okay?"

"Yes, of course," Drake mumbled, glad his lack of blood kept him from blushing.

Why do I feel like a schoolboy caught by the nuns for kissing a girl? She *hugged me.*

"Let's get him into the chair and out to the car." Dr. Cantora pointed at the wheelchair, her face a flat mask.

Drake thanked his lucky stars her interruption deflated his arousal as Bailey scrambled to help him up. His need to feed rose a little at her nearness, but it surged like a horse fighting the reins when the doctor shoved her shoulder under his other arm.

Damn, why does she smell so good? He closed his eyes and inhaled, reveling in her heat and chocolatey scent.

"Focus, please, Mr. MacGregor," the doctor barked and Drake jerked his eyes open.

"Yes, of course. Sorry."

They got him over the obstacle course of fallen books and dropped him into the chair. Dr. Cantora released him like he had the plague, retreating to the handlebars of the chair before he could read her expression. Bailey fussed over him, making sure he had his coat, hat and scarf wrapped around him, and promised to clean up the Archives room while he recovered.

"Call me if you need anything."

"I'll be fine, Bailey. Thank you for your help." Drake hunched into his jacket as Dr. Cantora wheeled him through the library. He ignored the curious stares of the few people still inside.

The doctor wheeled him out into the snowy night and the cold settled into him for the first time in centuries.

That's what I get for letting her distract me.

He shivered and stuffed his hands into his pockets as they rolled down the handicap ramp.

"The car is warm, Mr. MacGregor, and so is the clinic. We'll get you comfortable soon."

He suspected her ideas of comfortable differed greatly from his.

When they arrived at the car, she opened the door and warm air scented like her billowed into the frozen night. She offered her hand to help him into the car, but he brushed it rudely aside, mad at her for catching him with Bailey. And mad at himself for caring if she saw him.

"I can do it myself."

"Very well, Mr. MacGregor."

Her cold response dug the self-disappointment knife

deeper, but he lurched his way into the car and closed the door behind him. He had a little time to compose himself while she took care of the chair, but her scent only made his lust and arousal worse. By the time she opened the driver's door, his cock had hardened again and his hunger filled his mind with lascivious thoughts.

Silence encompassed the car ride to the clinic. Drake kept his eyes focused on the holiday décor festooning the street lights and traffic lights of Three Lakes as he dug his nails into his thighs. He hoped it would cool his thoughts toward the woman beside him. Her scent had changed a little with her irritation and sulfur edged out the spicy chocolate.

Good. Better for her to be angry with me than to encourage my lustful urges.

Dr. Cantora parked in front of the clinic and got out without a word. He heard her open the trunk as he scanned the dark building. Green holly garlands wound around the silver handrails for the front steps, their little red berries gleaming in the glow of the old fashioned walkway lamps. Drake jumped when the doctor jerked open the car door and he swore the little flakes of snow vaporized into steam when they hit her rigid shoulders. The scent of sulfur intensified and he hesitated.

"Do you need help to get out, Mr. MacGregor?"

"Oh, uh, no, thank you."

He swung his feet out, but only put weight on his good leg as he maneuvered into the chair she held. He almost lost his balance when dizziness assailed him, making him sway dangerously toward the sensually exotic doctor.

"Easy." She caught his elbow in a steady grip. "Let's get you into the clinic. I think you're going into shock."

Drake nodded and closed his eyes when he settled into the chair. He heard her slam the car door shut and felt the movement of the chair up the ramp, but he focused his attention on curbing the hunger raging against his willpower. If he wasn't careful, he'd attack the poor doctor and have to make reparations, not to mention the memory wipe. Pain and hunger surged and he clamped his hands over the armrests of the wheelchair to keep from grabbing the doc when she passed him to unlock the doors.

"Hang in there for me, Mr. MacGregor. Just a few more steps to get inside."

He opened his eyes to find the doctor's beautiful face damn near nose to nose with him and her scent flooded his awareness. A punch of lust overwhelmed his good sense and he rocked forward with the intent to kiss her delectable lips before he could stop himself.

Dr. Cantora's eyes narrowed and her mouth flattened into a hard line just before she pulled back out of reach.

"Don't you think you've had enough amorous embraces for one night, Mr. MacGregor?" She shook her head in disgust as she rose. "Given your state of shock, I can understand your unsteadiness, but I thought a man of your age would have better control over himself."

Her rejection left him reeling in a mixture of chagrin and relief as she threw the doors open and shoved him through. The heat of the building hit him like a wall, but the cold had settled inside. Hunger railed at him, screaming for him to leap out of this chair and tackle the doctor, consequences be damned. Drake gritted his teeth and fought his inner beast down.

The clinic sat dark and warm, but still smelled like antiseptic with the underlying taint of sickness. He hated clinics, their scents and ambiance always grating on his peace of mind. Tonight his usual distaste faded before the doctor's scent and heat. They were alone, all the other medical staff home safe in the face of the oncoming weather, and he was so hungry.

Dr. Cantora wheeled him into the X-ray room and turned on a light in the corner.

"It'll take a moment to warm up. Please remove your

pants so we can take an accurate X-ray to see the damage."

Drake gaped. "You want me to take off my pants?"

He'd never be able to hide his erection then.

"Yes."

She strode out of the room and he cursed under his breath. This day couldn't get any worse, unless he jumped Dr. Cantora and fucked her while he fed.

His inner beast cheered the idea.

Drake levered himself up to his one foot using the bench bed to keep him stable then balanced while he fiddled with his fly. His cock throbbed with arousal from the doctor's lingering scent and each brush of his fingers against the aching length eroded his grip on his inner beast.

He lost his balance as his hands shook from lack of fuel and he swore, fumbling with his zipper as he toppled against the bench. He released his pants to catch himself and they slid off his hips to tangle his ankles. With a cry of frustrated dismay, he collapsed to the side, unable to stop his fall.

Fuck, I'm so completely useless.

Expecting the impact with the floor, he closed his eyes and completely relaxed his body…And landed against something warm, soft, and spicy-scented.

"I've got you, Mr. MacGregor. You seem to be having a little trouble. Are you certain nothing other than your leg is broken?"

Drake wanted to answer, but the scent of her body so near to his nose and the blood under the silken skin of her throat destroyed his coherency. He wrapped his arms around her, throwing his weight against her chest, and nestled his nose at the base of her throat. Before his mind could stop his hunger, he'd driven his canines into her neck and filled his mouth with her sumptuous blood.

Two things registered to his hunger-fogged brain. The first was the unbelievable richness of her blood, richer than any blood he'd ever tasted. It filled his mouth like the legendary elixir of life and warmed his body from the inside out.

The second thing was a terrible snarl echoing through the room just before Dr. Cantora flung him bodily over the medical bench to crash into the metal shelves filled with lead aprons.

Drake opened his eyes to stare up at the woman towering over him, her eyes blazing with iridescent green fire as she held her neck with one taloned hand. Her canines showed clearly as she bared her teeth at him.

"What in the name of all that's holy do you think you're doing?"

CHAPTER TWO

Aliandra couldn't decide what she felt. Fury? Indignation? Lust? Arousal? Delight?

He bit me! He's a vampire. Oh Goddess, he's so sexy. Her thoughts cascaded rapid fire as she held her hand against her throat. The blood slowly stopped flowing beneath her talons, but her heartbeat only increased as her emotions banged around her skull like pinballs. She tried to take a few deep breaths to return to her human disguise, but her canines remained stubbornly long.

"I—I'm sorry, Dr. Cantora." Drake MacGregor stared at her, dazed and unsteady. He covered his mouth with one shaky hand. "I'm just so hungry and if you hadn't distracted me—"

"This is my fault?" She snarled and dug her claws into his lapels, jerking him nose to nose with her. "How is your biting me *my* fault?"

"If you hadn't distracted me, I wouldn't have forgotten to feed, and—"

"You haven't fed?" Aliandra hissed with disgust. "What kind of a vampire forgets to feed? Hellwinds, man, that's the stupidest thing I've ever heard."

She swung him around, pinning one hand behind his

back and propelled him across the room to one of the rolling doctor stools.

"Sit."

"Please, Doctor—"

"Sit!"

He sank down onto the cracked leather seat and eyed her warily, color returning to his cheeks as the blood he'd stolen worked its magic on him. She crossed her arms over her chest and clenched her jaws together to keep from tackling him and biting him back. Her body raged with a combination of arousal and excitement. He'd bitten her after nuzzling her shoulder like a dragon lover and her body wanted more.

But he's a vampire.

And she wanted more of him, more nuzzling, more biting. She scanned his body, belatedly realizing why he hadn't healed. He hadn't fed and all his energy had kept him upright, but he couldn't spare anything for physical repair. Mr. MacGregor needed blood and she was the closest donor.

"You need blood, don't you?"

"Yes, ma'am."

"That's why you didn't heal quickly tonight, right?"

He grimaced and nodded.

"Very well, Mr. MacGregor." She removed her coat and scarf, draping it over the exam table as she gathered her courage. "You may feed from me to get your strength up." She paused and looked over her shoulder at him. "You do know when to stop, correct?"

His mouth flattened with displeasure. "I *am* a mature sanguivore."

Aliandra snorted. "A *mature* sanguivore wouldn't let himself get in this position of being so weak."

Drake drew himself up to his full height and his expression smoothed out into regal impassiveness. He looked like a king unimpressed with the pleas of his subjects despite having to look up at her while seated. But she wasn't the one begging.

He's not begging, either. Dammit.

"Now is not the time to sit on your high horse, Mr. MacGregor." She tilted her head to hide the odd concern he'd decline to feed from her. "I've taken the Hippocratic Oath and you're in need of medical attention, even if it's to prevent starvation."

Drake's eyes flashed red and he unconsciously licked his lips, but he turned his face away as he shook his head.

"I can't do that, Doctor."

"You already have. I'm just giving you permission this time."

"I'm fine. What little blood I took from you has already helped."

His color did look better and he sat up straighter, but she suspected he was nowhere near satisfied. *Me, either.*

"It may have helped, but I can't let you leave and attack some innocent passerby if your hunger gets out of control again. I just thank the Goddess you attacked me instead of a human." She smiled at his look of shock. "What, did you think I was human?"

"Well...yes."

Aliandra laughed. "You and Kate. Your expression is priceless. I'm not human, Mr. MacGregor, I'm a dragon."

All the color he'd gained drained out of his face and he jerked to his feet, stumbling over the rolling stool in his haste. She reached for him, but he dodged clumsily in his attempt to get away. Unfortunately, his leg wouldn't hold his weight and he lurched against the wall beside the metal shelves.

"Mr. MacGregor—"

"Dear Goddess, please forgive me." His face morphed into a mask of horror. "I'm so sorry. I never meant any harm."

"Easy, Mr. MacGregor." Aliandra softened her voice,

wondering where his panic came from. "It's all right. No harm done and I'm offering you what you need. Let me help you sit down again."

"No, no, I swore I'd never do anything like this again." He tried to retreat, but the wall held him fast.

"I understand," she crooned, her hands up in a calming gesture. "Come sit back down and we'll find another solution. Please, Mr. MacGregor. You're injuring yourself worse."

He stared at her, his eyes glowing scarlet in the semi-darkness of the room, but he made no other move to retreat.

"Here, let me help you."

"No…no thank you, I can do it myself."

He rose painfully to full height and limped back to the stool. Aliandra's heart bled for him, but she stepped out of the way to give him his space. When he teetered dangerously to one side, she grasped his arm and helped him sit down. He hissed in surprise, but she held him until he settled.

"Now, before we do anything else, perhaps you'll let me look at your leg once more." Aliandra didn't want to spook him, but she needed to get her hands on his body again. "I want to be sure you haven't done more damage in your, uh, retreat."

Drake snorted with derision. "You mean my chicken-shit panic?"

"I would never say such things." She shot him a prim look, but couldn't hide her smile.

His chuckle turned into a hiss as she slid her fingers over the skin on his leg.

"Pain?"

"No." But his jaw remained clenched and his eyes glowed even brighter.

"I'd have to take an X-ray, but it *feels* like the bones have knit together. I can still feel muscle damage, however." She pulled her hands away and his shoulders relaxed. "You really need more blood."

"I'll get it when I go home."

"Are you going to go hunting?"

He said nothing, his gaze on his lap.

"I can't, in good conscience as a medical professional, allow you to leave here until I'm convinced of your general well-being."

"I can take care of myself, Doctor." Drake growled under his breath. "I'm not a child."

"I'm aware of that, but your recent disregard for your health suggests you might need some encouragement." When he opened his mouth to protest she held up one hand. "And you might attack someone and cause a scene that cannot be readily explained. I'm happy to offer you my blood for this evening and I'll announce to your assistant your injury was only a terrible strain, for which you'll need to wear a brace for a couple of days."

"I will not attack anyone."

"How can I be sure?" Aliandra raised an eyebrow. *He needs to take what he wants.* What they both wanted.

"Because I have excellent control."

"Oh, yes, I can tell from this healing bite mark on my neck." She snorted, rolling her eyes.

Drake snarled as he launched himself at Aliandra, slamming into her and pressing her against the medical table. Her inner dragon howled with triumph as he pressed his growing erection between her legs and stapled her hands to the bench behind her.

"If my control wasn't excellent, Dr. Cantora, I would have sunk my cock into your sweet-scented pussy and my teeth into your neck." He snarled his need, his eyes blazing crimson.

"Then do it, Mr. MacGregor."

He groaned and closed his eyes, but he dropped his lips to her throat once more and licked her, making her shiver. His teeth broke her skin and momentary pain exploded into erotic pleasure, eliciting a needy whimper.

"Oh, Goddess of all." She struggled against his grip. She had to touch him, to feel more of his body as he fed on her blood.

He grunted in agreement and kept siphoning her plasma in great swallows. Each pull ramped her arousal up higher, flooding her pussy with cream. She writhed against him and he rumbled another growl, grinding his cock harder into her belly.

He suckled a moment longer then pulled back to stare down at her, his face flushed with health and banked hunger.

"There, that's enough," he whispered, licking his lips clean of her blood.

"No, more. You need more." She tried to pull him down to her again. *I need more.*

"It's enough for me, Doctor."

"But it's not enough for me!"

Aliandra reared up and pushed him back then flipped him around until she pressed him against the medical table. He grunted in surprise and his eyes started to gleam again as she grinned with feral joy. If he wouldn't take her, she'd take him.

Dropping to her knees in front of him, she yanked down his black boxer briefs and admired the bold cock straining toward her from a nest of silver and black curls. His testicles drew up tight to his body, but when her breath caressed them, the skin flexed in reaction. Aliandra inhaled the spicy musk emanating from his balls and rumbled with appreciation.

He chuckled huskily. "You aren't going to eat me, are you, Doctor?"

"Depends on your definition of 'eat', Mr. MacGregor."

Aliandra grasped his hip with one hand, his cock with the other, and slid her mouth around his shaft all the way to the base. Drake hissed and threw his head back in pleasure as she massaged the silky skin of his dick. She took his response as encouragement and tightened her lips as she pulled back, allowing her canines to scrape along his shaft.

"Holy Goddess." Drake rocked his head forward and his eyes burned in the semi-darkness of the room. "You're diabolical, Doctor."

She chuckled and pulled back long enough to grin. "Not diabolical, draconic." She sucked him back in again.

Aliandra worked her lips and tongue over his hardened flesh, massaging and stroking as she savored the musky taste of his precum. Drake groaned and rocked his hips, and a pragmatic voice in the back of her mind noted his leg had healed.

She encircled the head of his cock with her tongue until he growled, his hands fastening on her biceps like steel bands. He yanked her to her feet, his penis springing out of her mouth with a loud *pop*. She growled back at him, but he'd already unfastened her jeans and shoved them down with her panties.

"I want to feel your hot pussy on my cock, Doc." He snarled as he pulled her to him.

"Excellent, Mr. MacGregor. My pussy wants your cock, now."

His eyes widened with amazed delight and he shoved his knees between her thighs, widening her legs until she straddled his hips.

"Take it, then, Doc."

She keened her pleasure as his hard shaft thrust up into her aching core. Fire flared through her body as he snarled and pulled back then thrust again, harder.

Pleasure swamped Aliandra and she forgot everything around her in her body's insistence on getting more. She gripped his shoulders, her hands shifting back into talons as she let go to the ecstasy of his hard loving. Drake's eyes blazed with crimson desire and his lips pulled back from his teeth just before he struck her throat again.

The combination of his fangs in her neck and his cock in her pussy threw her into an explosive orgasm, and she roared, digging her claws into his back. She opened her mouth and leaned forward, the urge to bite Drake as overwhelming as the cascading pleasure flooding through her.

The only thing that stopped her from following through was his sweater, plastered to his back from sweat and blood where her talons had broken his skin. Reality crashed into her just as Drake came, a long, drawn out moan seeping around his lips at her throat.

He's a vampire. He can't be my True Mate. Dragons only bit their mate-bonded partners, and only other dragons.

The pleasure from her orgasm drained away in the face of her revelation and bewildered chagrin took its place. She held still, trying to catch her breath and resisting the continued urge to bite the man between her legs.

I can't True-Mate a vampire.

Somehow, the logic didn't cool the need. The swipe of Drake's tongue on her skin made Aliandra jump and he raised his head to look at her, his expression full of satisfaction and health. But it immediately faded as he took in her face.

"Oh, dear Goddess, I'm sorry, Doctor." He smoothed her hair away from her face as contrition filled his expression. "I didn't hurt you, did I? I'm so sorry. There's no excuse for my behavior."

"Stop, Drake." She laid a hand over his lips. "You haven't hurt me and if you had, I still asked you to do what you did." She gave him a warm smile she didn't feel. "And you've fed, so you're well enough to get home without hurting yourself or others."

Aliandra pulled herself off him, but her body released him reluctantly. The slide of his skin against her softening pussy set off delicious aftershocks, but she retreated and tugged her jeans up from the floor. Her mind churned with the implications of her urge to bite the sexy vampire and for the first time in her eleven hundred years of life, she didn't know what to do.

She almost tripped over something on the floor and bent to pick up Drake's slacks, her uncertainty hitting her afresh. She turned to hand them to him, but he still sat on the medical table, his flaccid penis resting forgotten against his thigh. The scent of his seed and their lovemaking flavored the air, and she tried to ignore the spark of delight coursing through her.

Drake's expression destroyed any enjoyment of the moment. His features pinched with shame and disgust, and Aliandra hoped he wouldn't say anything too hurtful or scathing.

"I'm sorry." He clamped his lips shut as she cocked her head at him in warning. "Thank you for your help and for…the rest. I know you think it a mistake, as do I, but it was a pleasurable one and I'm grateful for it nonetheless."

She couldn't sort through her roiling emotions, so she settled behind her usual professional façade she used when telling a patient bad news.

"I'm glad you enjoyed it, Mr. MacGregor." She offered him his slacks. "I'll get you the brace to wear for a couple of days and I prescribe regular feedings to avoid both further injury and any erratic behavior."

Too bad they can't be with me.

"Thank you, Dr. Cantora."

Drake dropped his gaze, dressing, and she made herself leave the room to hunt for a leg brace. Bewilderment warred with grief, but she didn't know if she grieved for his rejection of her as a lover or bone-deep indication of being her True Mate. Fatigue dragged at her as she pawed through the medical supplies in the back room. The only adult brace she could find was black with a large red hearts emblazoned on it, but exhaustion stole her humor.

Aliandra found Drake seated on the medical table, lost in thought.

"Here's the brace. You should put it on now to maintain the illusion. I'll give you a ride home."

"Thanks." He raised an eyebrow. "Red hearts?"

"It was the only adult sized one I could find."

He grunted with some of his usual humor and strapped it on his leg. She watched the dim light catch on some of the silver in his hair and wished circumstances could be different. Why couldn't she find a nice dragon male to light her fire? What was so perfect about this distinguished, handsome, mature vampire?

Other than his sexy body, his gorgeous eyes, his tight ass, and his hard cock? Gee, let me think.

Drake stood up, straightening his clothes, and reached for his coat. Aliandra belatedly realized she'd never removed her shirt or bra and dismay flooded over her. Hellwinds, she'd behaved like a wanton whore. *Or a woman who knew what she wanted and refused to wait.* She'd go with the second statement.

She cleared her throat as she shrugged into her coat and scarf. "Ready?"

He nodded and limped after her, the brace restricting the motion of his leg. She grimaced, but said nothing. He had to look as if he'd been injured, no matter how uncomfortable. Aliandra locked the clinic doors behind him then hurried past him to unlock the car. Drake nodded his thanks and got in without a word.

She paused at the back of the car to let some of the wet snow cool her boiling emotions. She refused to think of what they'd done in the clinic as a mistake, but it certainly made life in Three Lakes a little more interesting. *How am I going to ignore my need for him?*

The drive to his home was steeped in silent tension. Discomfort radiated from every line in his body, but he never complained, staring out the side window at the snow dusted buildings. Aliandra tried to take an interest in the pretty view, but her mind kept churning over her recent revelation.

The jaunty awnings and cheery façade of the Ironwood Café appeared and she pulled over to the curb. The side door leading to the apartments above sat in darkness and she wondered if Drake preferred the hidden anonymity. *He's hiding from something.* She put the car in park and turned her gaze to his proud profile.

"Thank you for the ride." Drake offered her a wan smile as he opened the passenger door.

"Do you need help getting up to your apartment?"

"No, I'll be fine. Good night, Doctor."

"Good night, Mr. MacGregor."

She waited for him to enter the door leading to the apartments above the Café then turned her car and her mind toward home. Her teeth ached to bite Drake, but she shook her head against the need. She looked out at the night sky and wondered if she needed to take a flight just to relieve some of the desire coursing through her chest. *Just let it go and it'll fade.* She ignored the stench of her own internal lie.

CHAPTER THREE

Moonlight caressed Aliandra's back and wings as she sliced through the frigid winter air above the Warbler Peninsula, her mind stretching as much as her muscles. She'd been unable to sleep, though she'd been exhausted.

Blame it on the librarian. If he hadn't bitten me...

If he hadn't bitten her, she wouldn't have had sex with him, and wouldn't be in this quandary now.

How can he be my True Mate? How does that make any sense for species propagation?

She turned her gaze to the land sliding below her, following the ripples of the ancient terminal moraines left from the retreating ice sheets. Lights from human inhabitants sparkled like Christmas bulbs along their snaking ridges, connected by ribbons of community and asphalt.

Dropping closer to the roads below, the sounds of life intruded into her churning silence, and a large three-wheeled motorcycle chugged along the icy black blade cutting through the snowy land. Music blasted from the bike's speakers, belting out Bruce Springsteen's *Santa Claus is Coming to Town*. The rider sang along tunelessly, contentment in his voice.

Aliandra angled away, wishing she could find her own contentment in the winter skies above, but her frustration and despair followed her up like hunting dogs. *It's just not fair. Why did it have to be him?* Something about Drake MacGregor had intrigued her since Kate's wedding in late summer, and he seemed to watch her as much as she watched him. But she'd known he wasn't a dragon and she'd tried to stay away.

Because I want a family. She'd wanted children since before she was old enough to reproduce, but she'd focused on her career in medicine. The research and knowledge had been rewarding and demanding, but nothing soothed her soul like the thought of her own family.

She twisted in the air, spinning like a drill bit for a few seconds before she flared her wings out, stopping the tangled fear and despair from sucking her down into a quagmire. Feeling sorry for herself wouldn't get her anywhere. She'd just have to accept she'd never be a mother.

A keening wail filled the wind before she could stop it and her sorrow echoed in the heavens.

Everyone has dreams they don't fulfill in life.

Somehow the platitude didn't have any punch against her despair. Usually the wind and cool air brought her comfort when life's trials cut her deeply, but the clear, pre-dawn morning couldn't dispel the pall she felt in her heart.

Aliandra pivoted in the air over a wingtip, streaking low past a ridge of trees dangerously close to the frozen spires as if daring them to mark her. She squinted her eyes and held her wings taut, pushing herself faster and faster as if her actions would prove her worthy of what she couldn't have.

Actually, this just proves that you're stupid as well as unworthy of children.

The cold, hard thought jerked her back to reality and she banked upwards into a safer altitude, the wind whistling through the feathers behind her horns. She panted as she winged back toward town, working herself up so she'd be too tired to think when she got home. She clenched her feet talons into fists and soared gently into her spacious backyard. She landed with a gentle thump, dropping her wrists into the snow as she folded her wings. Even her tail felt heavy as she gathered her energy to shift back into her human disguise.

Why has the Goddess chosen a vampire to be my True Mate? And why has She chosen one who doesn't want me?

When she shifted into her human form, she felt even smaller and more alone than usual.

****

Drake stared up at the ceiling of his apartment and counted the flowers in the Rococo façade. He'd woken rested and energized, feeling physically on top of the world. But his guts churned with the memories of making love to Dr. Aliandra Cantora.

Actually, 'making love' wasn't accurate. He'd fucked her, and fucked her hard. It had been beyond any pleasure he'd ever experienced with a woman riding him and his body only craved more. The blood he'd ingested while they'd screwed fueled his body better and more efficiently than anything he'd ever consumed. He didn't even feel remotely hungry almost twelve hours later.

It has to be because she's a dragon.

Chagrin nailed him between the eyes and his balls shrank and tried to crawl up inside his body as his gut sank. *A real dragon, here in Three Lakes.* Back before he'd moved to the New World, he'd always assumed they were mythical beasts, stories constructed from the bones unearthed in China or Mongolia. Never a real creature living among the humans and other Elder Races. When he'd been knighted in the Order of the Dragon by his father, dragons had been an idea of purity and strength, something meant to be revered. Back then, it had been an honorable knightly Order.

Until he'd sullied it.

Drake had spent the last four centuries trying to make reparations for his actions in Wallachia. He didn't think he'd ever make up for the damage he'd done.

And now he'd dishonored a dragon by taking advantage of her. A real dragon.

He groaned and rolled over onto his stomach, hiding his head in the pillow. In terms of bad decisions, this had to be his worst in at least two hundred years. He tried to shove her out of his mind, to focus on getting out of bed and starting on his day, but images of Aliandra in an elegant raw silk dress the color of the sunset overwhelmed his mind's eye.

Aliandra had worn the dress to Kate's wedding celebration and Drake hadn't been able to take his eyes off her feminine curves. She'd raised her glass of champagne while a drunk guest gave a generic toast to the newlyweds and he'd swallowed his tongue as the bodice tightened over her full breasts.

Drake had felt like a lemur in mating season, ready to screw anything that walked by. Only a badly sung serenade managed to break him of his lecherous spell enough to leave without jumping her.

So you waited to do it in the clinic instead. Smooth move, idiot.

Fortunately, he wouldn't have to see her much with her duties as a doctor keeping her busy. His job in the Archives kept him inside and away from the public most of the time. He wouldn't have to see her at all, especially now that she'd given him the brace. He'd just remove it in a week when he'd 'healed' and have Bailey return it to the clinic.

Coward.

Shaking his head, Drake swung his feet over the side

of the bed and forced himself to face the day. *And ignore my cock.* His morning routine usually included a "tomato" protein shake and a thorough mouth cleansing to disguise the scent of blood, but he bypassed both in favor of coffee and a bagel from the Ironwood Café downstairs. He didn't need food at his age, but it felt good to be "normal" and interact with his neighbors in town. Bundling up against the cold and weak winter sunlight, he descended to the street outside.

"Good morning, Drake." Iris Maple waved as he walked in. She cocked her head to one side and eyed him speculatively. "You look well this morning."

Drake raised an eyebrow. "When I usually look like death warmed over?"

"No, no." She laughed. "You just look particularly good this morning." She handed him a menu when he took one of the booths away from the windows. "What can I get you?"

He hung his coat and scarf on the little hooks bolted to the booth and sat down. "Bagel with garlic cream cheese and coffee."

Iris grunted with surprise. "You must be feeling good. I'll get right on that." She sauntered away, the ends of the scarf covering her head brushing her shoulder blades.

Drake suspected her head must be almost bald by this time of year. As Queen of the local Dryad Garden, she changed with the seasons. Her hair grew in pale blond in the spring, darkened to rich gold in the summer, and burnished into fiery rust in autumn before falling out for winter. The humans in town thought she preferred to dye it throughout the year, an explanation she encouraged to hide her species.

Iris returned with a coffee decanter. "Oh, by the way, a guy stopped in here asking about the Library. Apparently, he's a researcher studying families emigrating here from somewhere 'across the pond.' I told him to talk to you in the Archives when you got in."

Normally the news of a visiting researcher piqued Drake's professional interest and he'd finish whatever he was doing to go see who'd arrived. But something in Iris's description sent a chill up his spine and he scanned her expression for the source of the warning.

"Oh? I'll head over there after my breakfast."

She nodded tight-lipped.

"Something wrong with this researcher, Iris?"

"I don't like him, Drake." She let her gaze to scan the patrons of the Café. "There's something not quite right about him, even if he did *seem* normal enough with his son and all."

"Son?"

"Yes, a little boy about five years old. Poor, little sapling looks like he's been dragged all over hell and gone, but he was polite enough." Iris shook her head. "Just keep your eyes open around that man. He carried the scent of forest fires and blight."

Drake considered the dryad Queen's warning as he sipped his coffee and watched a new layer of snow fall outside the windows of the café. Iris rarely took exception to anyone. She reacted slowly and patiently like any tree, often weathering the worst to find the best in people. But if she already had her bark up, he knew he should heed her remarks.

Drake finished his meal and left a generous tip for Iris then wrapped his scarf around his neck as he returned to the blustery sidewalk outside. The weather playing havoc kept Main Street empty and he hurried his steps toward the library, his mind churning. Iris's warning worried him.

After the assassination attempt by a fanatical religious organization the previous summer on Kate Blackamber, their resident *Morukai* shaman, the Elder Races community had become more watchful. Drake recalled the assassin calling himself a blade of God or something. *It could be nothing.*

His own thought made him scoff. Iris wouldn't have warned him if she didn't believe a real threat existed. Huffing a breath in the snow-filled air, he increased his uneven pace until he reached the doors of the library.

The heat inside slammed into Drake as the doors closed behind him. Condensation fogged the windows and the scents of pine and cinnamon assaulted his nose from the holiday decorations Bailey had hung up. Another scent, something slightly putrid, lay hidden beneath the holiday cheer and he coughed as he limped toward the Archives.

"Oh, Mr. MacGregor, I didn't expect you here today." Bailey looked up from the reference desk. "How is your leg?"

"It's not as bad as we feared." He patted his thigh. "Just a really bad sprain and bone bruise. I'll have to wear the brace for a few days, but it's already feeling better."

More than better. He hadn't felt this good in centuries and he had yet to feel his usual hunger.

Don't get to attached to it, fool. It's not likely you'll get more dragon blood any time soon.

"Oh, I'm so glad to hear that." Bailey smiled in relief. "There's a gentleman here visiting from some university in…" She trailed off with a frown then waved her hand in dismissal. "Chapel Hill, North Carolina, I think he said. I'm sure he'll tell you all about it. He's in your office. I told him I didn't think you were coming in, but he insisted."

"Did he give you his name?" Drake's mind returned to Iris' warning.

"Dr. Viggo Lance. And he brought his son Thomas with him."

"Did he?" Drake turned his head toward his office. "I'd best go and greet them, then."

"Do you need any help?"

"No, thank you, Bailey. I'll be fine."

Drake patted the counter in farewell and limped toward

his office in the Archives. The unpleasant scent became stronger as he approached the Archives and he wrinkled his nose in distaste. Had he left something to rot in his office?

Shuffling through his door, he spied a tall, slender, graying man perusing the books on the shelves nearest the door to the Archives. Movement opposite the desk caught Drake's eye and a small, dark-haired boy with silver-gray eyes swung his feet back and forth while he sat on one of the high-backed chairs. The boy froze when he saw Drake, cocking his head to one side in a way that reminded Drake of Dr. Cantora.

"May I help you?" Drake asked as he stepped into full view.

The man spun and braced himself for evasive action before straightening up and smoothing his sweater. He smiled in greeting, but a tingle of unease skittered up Drake's spine as he met the man's gaze. The eyes were cold and calculating, hard with no compassion.

"Yes, you must be the Archivist, Mr. MacGregor." Despite his officious look, the man's voice was smooth and warm. "My name is Dr. Viggo Lance and this is my son, Thomas."

"What can I do for you, Dr. Lance?" Drake disrobed from his coat and scarf, careful never to turn his back to his visitor. Like Iris had mentioned, something seemed off about him.

"I'm hoping for some historical knowledge help." Lance took a seat in the other chair beside the boy. "I've been studying the emigrations of people from Scotland to the United States, tracking where they've settled and what sorts of genetic traits they've passed on to their descendents."

"Are you a geneticist, Dr. Lance?"

"Not per se, more of a genealogist with an interest in genetic code and how certain traits seem to pervade a given population."

That seemed reasonable enough, but Drake couldn't shake the feeling he'd missed something.

"Why families from Scotland?" He sat behind his desk and pulled his tablet out of its case, powering it up.

"A few of them show a remarkable longevity in most, if not all, of their members and I'm tracking them to see if it's possible to duplicate or pass on such longevity to the population at large." Drake could hear the enthusiasm in the doctor's voice.

"I see. Do you have the names of these families?"

"Yes and no." Dr. Lance leaned forward with his elbows on his knees, a frown creasing his brow. "As you know, names change with marriages and adoptions, but I have some leads that have brought me here to Three Lakes."

Drake nodded as he gathered his thoughts. "Where are you from, Dr. Lance?" He scrolled through the Archives database, looking for Scottish names in the registry.

"Chapel Hill, North Carolina."

The boy beside the professor shifted in his seat and Drake smelled the half-truth, but kept his expression neutral.

"A long way to come for in-person research. You could have called or emailed me rather than travel at this time of year."

Dr. Lance sighed and bowed his head. "I'm on sabbatical from the University after my wife died this summer. I thought it best for me and Thomas to get away."

"Ah," Drake grunted, though he could think of far better places to go than the Warbler Peninsula in late November. "I'm sorry for your loss."

"We just wanted to be free of the memories for a while." Dr. Lance nodded, his shoulders slumping.

"I can imagine. The death of your wife must have been fairly traumatic."

"It was. A drunk college student hit her on her way

home. She was killed instantly."

Sorrow etched the professor's face, but his voice was more matter-of-fact than grieving. Drake's gaze slipped over to Thomas, but the boy had turned his head and picked at a loose thread in his sweater.

"Again, I'm sorry. I've cued up the familial records of the past two hundred years into that terminal there on the table behind you. You should be able to access all the births, deaths, marriages, divorces, and emigrations of Three Lakes' European and Old World population there."

"European population?"

"Yes. The Cree peoples have never kept records with us so there are only accurate records of the people from across the Atlantic who settled here."

"Thank you, Mr. MacGregor. I greatly appreciate your help." Dr. Lance rose and held out his hand for Drake to shake.

Drake took his hand and immediately wished he hadn't. While the man's grip was firm, the dryness of the hard calluses across the palm shot a warning through Drake's awareness. He released him quickly.

"I'm happy to help." Drake hesitated and looked pointedly at the boy. "What will Thomas do while you research?"

"I told him he could peruse the library on his own. You do have a Children's Section, correct?"

"Of course. I'll be happy to show him where it is."

"Thank you again, Mr. MacGregor." Dr. Lance turned to Thomas. "Go with Mr. MacGregor now and I'll see you in a few hours, all right?"

"Yes, Viggo," the boy replied dutifully.

"Very good." Lance focused his attention on the computer.

Drake locked his computer terminal and grabbed his tablet, grateful the Archives remained locked until he opened them. Something about the good Dr. Lance made

Drake want to hide as much as possible from him. Not his usual reaction to visiting researchers.

Iris's warning is getting to me.

"Come with me, Thomas. We have some great books about all sorts of things. What are you interested in?" Drake ushered the boy out into the main library.

"I like airplanes and boats."

"Well, we have a big selection of airplane books, starting with the first plane to ever fly." Drake's shoulders loosened with every step further from his office. "Do you know the name of the first airplane?"

"No, sir."

"It was the Wright Flyer, built by Orville and Wilbur Wright in 1903 from Kitty Hawk, North Carolina, where you're from."

"I'm not from North Carolina," Thomas whispered, glancing back over his shoulder toward the Archives. "I'm from Scotland. Dr. Lance adopted me after the death of his wife."

Surprise and unease shot down Drake's spine. "Where are your parents?"

"Dead." Thomas's voice was flat.

For one moment, Drake wanted to ask if Dr. Lance had killed them, but thought better of it before the words passed his lips.

That's a stupid idea. Just because the guy unnerves you doesn't mean he's a killer. Get a hold of yourself, MacGregor.

"I'm sorry, Thomas. I know what it's like to lose someone close."

"It's okay, Mr. MacGregor. I like your name and you're nice. Are you from Scotland?"

"No, but my family name comes from there." That was a half-truth. The family origins of the name he'd taken came from Scotland.

Thomas looked up at him with his odd silver-gray eyes

and Drake felt as if the boy could see more of him than Drake liked to share. But Thomas smiled and nodded. Sadness tinged the smile, but Drake sensed it was the first time the boy had shown the expression in a long time.

"How old are you, Thomas?"

"I'm…four, almost five."

"You're very well-spoken for a four year old."

"Viggo taught me a lot of words this summer. But he's not interested in airplanes. I want to know more about airplanes."

"Okay, Thomas."

"Can you call me Tom?" The boy looked up at Drake with barely concealed frustration. "Thomas isn't my name, but Viggo insisted and I don't want to make him mad. He's already mad enough."

Probably from the death of his wife. But that didn't feel completely accurate.

"Sure, I can call you Tom, if you prefer."

"My mum called me Tom."

"Very well, Tom it is."

Drake drew Tom over to a low, round table painted in multi-colored polka dots. Despite its whimsy in an otherwise serious place, Drake liked the bright spots Bailey had painted on the table's surface and the matching small plastic chairs. Drake pulled out a blue one for Tom and lowered himself gracelessly into a yellow one, his braced leg sticking out awkwardly.

"Right over there, between that bright red book and the one with a black and white checkered spine is all the airplane books we have in this section," Drake explained, pointing at the shelves below the big picture window. "Can you read, Tom?"

"Yes, sir."

Drake nodded, surprised. "Very good. Why don't you go and select a few books, and we'll look at them together."

"What happened to your leg, Mr. MacGregor?" Tom asked as he investigated the books.

"I fell in my office and bruised the bones of my leg pretty badly." Drake sighed with a rueful smile. "It'll be better in a few days."

"Why didn't it heal fast?" The boy didn't look at him, but Drake froze as surprise worked its way through him.

"I'm sorry?"

"Why didn't your leg heal fast?" Tom turned with several book in his arms. "I thought people like you heal right fast."

Drake eyed the boy warily when he returned to the table and Tom gave him a level silver-gray stare filled with guarded curiosity.

"People like me?" *Who is this kid?*

Tom opened his mouth to answer, but stopped short when he realized what he'd said and grimaced, looking down at the books on the table.

"I'm sorry, sir. That was rude of me. I didn't mean to say something inappropriate. Please forgive me." The boy's shoulders hunched a little as if he expected to be cuffed.

Drake's unease increased. Tom's response set off warning bells in his head. It sounded as if he'd been reprimanded before and harshly so. Drake's anger kindled and he did his best to keep it out of his expression as he smiled.

"No, no, Tom, I'm not offended by your question." He opened the topmost book. "I was just curious what you meant. No harm done. Come, let's look at these books. What do you like best about airplanes?"

The moment passed and Tom relaxed enough to talk about his love of flight. Flight details like Bernoulli's Principle and fixed-wing aerodynamics filled the space between them, but Drake's mind replayed the interactions between Dr. Lance and his "son". Something struck him as wrong about the connection between the two and he already regarded the professor with unease.

This kid is special in some way. I'll just have to wait to see what more I can do to help him.

The morning whiled away and Drake found himself enjoying Tom's keen observations about aircraft and the changes in them over time. He managed to coax the boy out of his reserved shell and smiles crept across Tom's face more often as the morning passed.

At one point, Drake heard the front doors open while they discussed thrust and why it was important to flight, but Tom stiffened into a stillness so complete, Drake would have thought him a vampire. Drake almost asked him what was wrong when a familiar delicious scent hit him and he turned his head to look for the source.

He found her standing at the reference desk speaking to Bailey, who pointed in his direction. Dr. Cantora turned her own head and met his gaze. The sight of those deep teal eyes hit him like a punch to the gut, equal parts elation and dread.

Oh, Goddess, I can't see her now.

Oh, Goddess, I'm so glad she's here.

His conflicting thoughts must have done something odd to his face because she cocked her head as a frown lowered her brows when she approached the children's section. He belatedly remembered to stand in the presence of a lady and started to scramble to his feet, but she smiled and waved him down. Then she stopped as if she'd run into a wall.

What's wrong?

He followed her line of sight and found Tom's silver-gray gaze trained on her. Both the boy and woman studied each other for a few microseconds before they reanimated as if nothing had happened. Tom fiddled with the books on the table, rearranging them as if bored with the top one. Dr. Cantora resumed her approach and pasted a smile on her face, though her eyes showed uncertainty in their depths.

"Good morning, Mr. MacGregor." At the sound of her sultry voice, Drake's cock stirred and his mind filled with the memories of taking her.

Down, boy! She's not for you.

"Good morning, Dr. Cantora. What brings you here today?"

"I came to check on you and see how your leg is doing. Any extraneous pain?"

Even though she asked him questions, her gaze remained on the boy as she circled the table and sat down in a green chair across from Tom. The boy didn't look up, studiously ignoring her.

"No, ma'am. No. It seems to be healing very well, thank you," Drake replied, curious about the interaction between the dragon and the boy.

"Who is your young friend here, Mr. MacGregor?" Aliandra's face showed only polite curiosity, but her scent had shifted from sun-baked mesquite to sharp pine as her interest intensified.

"Oh, forgive me. This is Tom Lance, visiting from North Carolina. Tom, I'd like to introduce Dr. Aliandra Cantora del Viento."

The boy finally looked up at Aliandra and slowly reached out to shake her hand. She smiled gently and took his offering, jerking just a little when they touched. Tom froze again and several seconds ticked by as they stared at each other. Drake didn't know what passed between them, but Aliandra's smile broadened and Tom's shoulders relaxed, his own shy smile peeking out.

"Very nice to meet you, Tom." Aliandra nodded. Drake heard sorrow and yearning in her voice.

"Very nice to meet you, too, Dr. Cantora." The boy sighed and wiggled just a little.

"You can call me Aliandra, Tom." She released his hand reluctantly.

"Do you like airplanes, Aliandra?" Tom rose from his

chair and dragging a book over the seat next to her.

"You know, I do like airplanes. What do you like best about them?" She turned her full attention on the boy and stared at the book as he explained.

Drake found himself an unexpected observer to the drama playing out before him, completely forgotten by the participants. His heart swelled at the look of Aliandra doting on this young, neglected boy, and he had a sudden vision of her as his wife and Tom as his son, reading other books. His family.

A yearning so deep and strong damn near stopped his heart and tossed him to the floor. Amazement slammed into him and he inhaled to fill lungs too tight for breath.

What is wrong with me? I can't have *a family ever again.* Especially not Aliandra Cantora or Tom Lance. Besides his past, he was a vampire to her dragon. *And Tom's human.* At least, he thought he was human, but he'd never seen Aliandra react that way over other children. *As if you've spent that much time with her.*

But the yearning remained so strong his eyes clouded with tears and he had to look away before he betrayed his emotions. Clearing his throat, he struggled to his feet and smiled awkwardly down at the other two as they looked up at his motion.

"Thank you for coming by, Doctor. Would you be willing to watch over Tom for a bit?" He straightened his sweater in an effort to reclaim his composure, but his heart hammered. "I have a few things I must get done today."

"Of course, Mr. MacGregor." Aliandra nodded with a distracted smile. "I'd be happy to read with Tom for a little while."

"Thank you, Doctor. Please excuse me."

Drake turned and shuffled away as fast as his braced leg allowed from the tempting dreams he knew could never come to be, his heart aching with every step.

CHAPTER FOUR

Aliandra felt Drake's retreat like a blade to her chest and hurt stabbed through her heart. *Why does he want to get away from me so much?* Then she mentally shook her head. It didn't matter. He couldn't give her what she truly wanted and he feared dragons or something associated with them. *Let it go.*

She turned her attention back to the boy beside her and found him watching her with thoughtful expression on his face. When she'd first come in, she hadn't felt his presence at all. *That's because you were too caught up in Drake MacGregor.* But as soon as she saw Tom, she knew she shared bloodlines with him, however distant.

"I think he likes you, Aliandra," Tom said softly.

"Do you think so? He's always trying to get away from me whenever I see him." She laughed bitterly.

"Well, *I* like you." Tom puffed out his chest. "You're just like my mum."

The words *my mum* unleashed all her yearning for a child of her own and she had to shove her recent grief at the loss of her dream down deep. She knew he hadn't meant her to take it as if she was his mother, but her heart knocked her ribs with sorrow anyway.

"How am I like your mother?"

Tom glanced around them to be sure no one stood nearby then leaned close to her with the intent to whisper. She dropped her head beside his.

"You're a dragon." His words flowed no louder than a sibilant hiss, but she caught them clearly, her instinct validated.

"So are you, aren't you?"

The young dragonet nodded, a secret smile wreathing his lips.

"Where are your parents, Tom?"

Bone-deep sorrow washed across his features.

"They died."

Fury seared her breath from her lungs and she had to close her eyes and clench her fists for a moment before she did something wholly dragon and torch the building around her. *How could that happen? We're tough and so good at hiding from anyone's evil ignorance.*

"I'm sorry to hear that, Tom." She tried to smile. "Who is taking care of you now? Drake?"

"Drake?"

"Sorry, Mr. MacGregor, I meant."

"Oh, no." Tom dragged a nervous finger over the image of an F-15 Eagle flying upside down. "No, I was adopted by a human named Dr. Viggo Lance. He's doing research here. Are you a professor, too?"

"No, I'm a medical doctor. I try to help people. Where did Dr. Lance find you, Tom?"

"Inverness, Scotland. How do you help people? Do you find them families?"

Aliandra's throat closed and she had to shake her head a few times before she could speak around the lump the size of the Andes. *Dear Goddess, why is everything reminding me of what I can't have?*

"I'm not that kind of doctor." She squeaked, her voice so rough it felt like she spoke through gravel. She cleared her throat much like Drake had done. "I'm a medical doctor."

Tom sighed with disappointment. "I wish you could find me a family."

"What about Dr. Lance? Isn't he your adopted father?"

Tom shrugged. "He took me from home and feeds me. I guess that's enough."

Aliandra wanted to snarl. *How could anyone ignore this child and treat him so indifferently?* If Tom was hers, she'd spend every free moment she could teaching him everything he needed to know to be a dragon.

"But he's not like you. He's not a dragon." Tom stroked the book and the glossy pages.

Precisely. I wish Tom was mine to care for.

Now where had that thought come from? In her life as a medical doctor, she didn't really have time to take care of a child, not the way a child deserved. But she wanted it more than she'd ever wanted anything other than Drake MacGregor. If she couldn't have Drake, perhaps she could have Tom.

And while we're wishing, could I have a cave full of crystals and a whole herd of llamas to feed on?

Her sarcasm saved her from falling to a pit of despair deeper than the one in that funny fantasy movie she'd seen almost three decades earlier.

"Not many are like you and me. I've been meaning to ask. How old are you, Tom?"

"I'm almost…" He frowned and she waited for him to decide which scale to use. "Five. I'm almost five."

Almost to his first century. Probably several decades older than the man who'd adopted him. "And what's your full name?"

Tom met her gaze and bit his lip. "Tomarrion Shearwinds."

She'd never heard of the Shearwinds family, but she wondered if others in her clan had. Despite the need to find his relatives, she resisted reaching out. *He's mine to care for. He's here and I want him.* She shoved her thoughts to the side to think on later.

"I see you like reading."

"I like the pictures best of all."

Aliandra grinned. "Me too."

"Is that why you came to the library today?" Tom turned the pages, pausing on the A-10 Warthog.

"Actually, I came to check on Mr. MacGregor. I'm sure you noticed he'd hurt his leg."

"Yes. He said he fell and bruised his bones."

"That's right. I just wanted to make sure he was okay." *And see his handsome face and smell his delicious scent.*

"He smells like he will be okay, but you can go check if you want to." Tom shrugged and turned another page.

Aliandra stared at the boy for a few moments, trying to decipher what he'd meant. "Are you sure you'll be okay on your own for a little while?"

"Oh, yes. Viggo lets me be alone a lot. I think he needs a lot of time to himself, too."

She ground her molars, but she offered him a smile and patted his shoulder.

"All right. I'll go make sure Mr. MacGregor is truly doing okay." She paused a moment and smiled at him. "If it's okay with Dr. Lance, you're welcome to come visit the clinic. I can't promise I won't be busy, but you're welcome to stop by. I'm sure Mr. MacGregor could show you where it is."

Tom gave her a sweet smile. "I'll remember. Thank you."

"My pleasure. It was very nice to meet you, Tom."

"Aliandra?"

"Yes?"

"Will you come back to the library again?"

Tom's request melted her heart and tears threatened. "Yes." She cleared her throat. "Yes, I can do that when I don't have to work at the clinic."

"Okay. Good."

"See you soon." She waved and retreated before her yearning tears spilled down her cheeks. How could one little boy affect her so strongly?

Because you desperately want a family of your own and here's an orphaned dragonet? An orphaned dragonet who's family she should try to contact. She sighed and promised herself she'd send a message to her family back home. Honor demanded she make the effort. Taking a deep breath, she hunted for Mr. MacGregor.

She found him in his office, studiously ignoring the other man in the room. She paused at the doorway, hesitating to intrude. *What I am really doing here?* The man looked fine. *More than fine. Hawt.* He only wore the brace for show.

Squaring her shoulders, she shoved her misgivings aside and entered the Archives. Two things hit her at the same moment. First, Drake's scent seemed spiced with frustration and tension, but he sat at apparent ease behind his desk. And second, the smell wafting off the other occupant of the room made her want to hurl the rare steak she'd eaten for breakfast that morning.

Holy Mother of all, what is that stench?

She coughed and both men looked up as she clapped a hand over her mouth in chagrin.

"Oh, please, excuse me." Aliandra waved her hand in front of her face. "Something went down the wrong way."

"Is there something I can do for you, Dr. Cantora?" Drake's voice held icy courtesy.

She drew herself up, anger kindling. What was his problem?

"I came to check on the progress of your injury, Mr. MacGregor. I trust everything is fine."

"Yes, thank you, Doctor."

"No extra pain or discomfort?"

"No, ma'am."

"Very well. Then I'll bid you good-day." She nodded to him sharply and spun, striding away from his disdain as fast as she could without running.

She knew he didn't want to be with her, but she hadn't expected him to be rude. Anger and hurt roiled in a morass of emotion and she clenched her jaw against frustrated tears.

What is wrong with me? I better get it together before I see any patients today.

Aliandra wrapped her coat tightly around her and stepped out into the gray, cold day, leaving the library's warm scents, and the sexy librarian, behind.

****

Drake cursed inwardly, but only dropped his head to continue working on his tablet. Not that he saw anything other than Aliandra's perfect backside or the way the light glinted in her hair. Or the way the anger flushed her face when he'd dismissed her so harshly.

Fuck.

He hadn't wanted her to leave, but the idea of Dr. Lance taking an interest in her curdled his stomach. He didn't want the professor to know anything about his lovely dragon lady. The man set his teeth on edge.

"Awful nice of her to come check on you like that," Dr. Lance said, flipping through his notes. "She do that for everyone?"

Drake adjusted his wire rimmed glasses he wore for show and smiled briefly. "Yes. That's the way folks are in this town. We look out for each other."

"Must be nice to have a lady like that looking after you. Tilly used to do that for me when she was alive."

The sorrow sounded real enough, but Drake still got an uneasy chill from the words.

"I best go see how your son is doing. Excuse me."

Dr. Lance didn't even nod as Drake limped out of the Archives. *What is wrong with this man that he doesn't even take the time to be concerned with his son?*

Drake breathed a sigh of relief when he shuffled into Bailey's pine and holly scented domain. His negative reaction to the man in his office had colored everything about the day and he tried recall his politeness. Bailey smiled at him from the reference desk, but her sweet face only sparked his memory of Aliandra's expression when she'd left, and his mood plummeted again.

Dammit. He should find her and apologize, but he didn't think she'd like being interrupted during her work at the clinic. And what would he say to her?

"Sorry, Doc, I didn't want that guy to know anything about you, or even look at you, because he's creepy and I'm liable to rip his head off for doing it." Yeah, not likely.

He passed two teen-aged boys flipping through an art book and caught the sounds of techno music blaring from a dangling earbud.

"Dude, what's that?" The boy with the striped tuque pointed to a photo.

"It's a statue, duh." The boy with the earbuds grunted when his friend thumped his shoulder with a fist.

"Not that. *That.*" Both the lads looked closer and Drake couldn't help but stop.

"*That* is a mala, a Hindu rosary," Drake said. The boys jumped a little. "What are you listening to?"

"Moby, *Mysterious Ways*," Tuque said.

"That's *Extreme Ways*, dork."

"Ah, well, could you turn it down? We are in a library." Earbud reached into his pocket and the music stopped. "Thank you. Did you know that statue is supposed to send real prayers up to the Creator?"

"Really?"

"Yes, that's why someone draped a rosary around the

outstretched hand. It's the same idea with prayer flags in Tibet."

"What, you just 'flag' God down?" Earbud snickered.

"That's a good analogy. Each one has a special prayer and the wind carries it to God's ears."

"Wow, that's cool. Do you think it would work here in Michigan?" Tuque asked.

"I think anything's possible."

"I'm gonna do that for my mom. Do you know where I can find some of those flags?" Tuque looked up at Drake earnestly.

"You could probably make them yourself." The boy didn't look very impressed. "But if you truly want official flags, I'd go visit Gemini's Store and ask her if she can order some for you."

"At the grocery store?" Earbud's expression filled with derision.

"Amazing things can be found at Gemini's place. Don't knock it until you've tried it."

"Thank you." Tuque left the book in his friend's hands. "I'll see you later, dude."

Earbud just grunted and dropped the book. He stuck the earbud back into his ear and the music resumed as he trudged out of the library. Drake shook his head, picked up the art book, and left it on the circulation desk for Bailey to shelve.

Maybe he should make some prayer flags to the Goddess in supplication of forgiveness for his transgressions. He could add prayers for love and family and...*And what? I'm an old grizzled vampire with nothing to offer but a sketchy history.*

Drake continued his path through the library, trying to take comfort in the cozy environment and the quiet intensity of the patrons. Tom still sat with the airplane books strewn around him on the polka dot table, but he stared out the window, watching people walk by the library. His body language screamed sorrow and resignation, as if he waited for something he believed would never come.

"Tom, are you all right?"

The boy jerked and looked around as if he'd been caught doing something naughty. When he saw Drake, relief flooded his face and he nodded.

"Yes, Mr. MacGregor."

"Did you enjoy reading the books?"

"Yes, sir. Aliandra helped me with some of them. I hope she comes back to the library soon."

Drake sighed and sat down in one of the kiddie chairs beside the book-strewn table. "Me, too, Tom. She's pretty busy. But I hope she will."

"I like her. She's special." He looked Drake in the eye with subtle intensity that had the hair on the back of his neck rising in warning. "Did you make her mad?"

Drake sighed and dropped his chin. "Yes, I do believe I did."

"Why?"

How could he explain to a five year old? "I wasn't as grateful as I should've been." He paused again as a new idea occurred to him. "Shall we go find her and apologize?"

The boy didn't hesitate. "Yes. Where should we go?"

"Anywhere but here," Drake muttered, gathering up the books. "I'll bet she's at the clinic. Get your coat and we'll go."

"Okay. She said I could come visit if it was okay with Viggo. She said you could show me where it is."

"Did she?" Irrational jealousy rose within him. Sad, to be jealous of a child. "That's wonderful. We'll let Dr. Lance know we're going. Seem fair?"

Tom nodded solemnly as he helped shelved the books then followed behind Drake. As they approached the Archives, Tom's demeanor became more and more subdued, losing the luster and sparkle he'd shown when alone. Drake's tension rose as soon as they entered the office, the odor of the man working there making his hackles rise.

Tom approached the man seated behind the research terminal, his shoulders straight, but his head down. Drake grabbed his coat, scarf, and hat, watching out of the corner of his eye. The boy waited patiently for the man to notice him, but the seconds stretched into minutes, and Drake's disgust rose at each passing moment.

When there was nothing left for him to gather or shut down or put on, Drake cleared his throat and stood in front of the work table.

"Dr. Lance, I have a need to go out for a time."

"Very good, Mr. MacGregor. I shall be fine here." Lance didn't even look up from his research.

"That's good. Thomas has asked to come with me and I have no problem with his company." Drake gritted his teeth. "Is it all right with you if he accompanies me?"

The man looked up, his expression a mask of frustration until Drake's words sank in. Then his face cleared into a benevolent smile.

"Oh, yes, of course. Be sure to bundle up, Thomas, and mind your manners."

"Yes, sir." Tom's expression remained shuttered.

"Have a good time." Lance turned back to his computer without another look.

Tom didn't waste any time. He grabbed his hat and coat, and darted out of the office.

"I'll have him back in no more than an hour or so." Drake spoke to Lance's bowed head.

"That's fine. Take your time."

Drake nodded and remembered to take his tablet with him. For some reason, he didn't trust it in the same room with the "doctor." He was just as happy to leave the man, and his noxious scent, behind as Tom.

****

Viggo breathed a sigh of relief as the archivist and the brat left the room. He didn't have time for trifling matters and he'd only brought Thomas with him to stave off suspicion over his research. *Soon.* He consoled himself with the knowledge his research neared completion. This little Podunk town was the last step in his long journey toward fulfilling his quest.

The Sword of God had charged him with finding the worst creature ever to sully the soil of Earth and he'd diligently followed the clues. He'd been out of touch with his Brothers for a long time, but his determination paid off. The threads of his quest all led here and while the clues to his quarry remained couched in innuendo and veils, he'd deciphered their slippery tracks.

At least the little brat he'd picked up in Scotland remained quiet and out of the way. He'd been bawling when Viggo found him after the massacre of the Shearwinds family, those shape-changing demons. Viggo would've left him to starve if he hadn't needed a good cover story when an old biddy in the village asked who he was. He hadn't wanted the responsibility of a child, but the brat had proved useful for getting into places a single man found resistance, even a man as distinguished as himself.

But he'd dump the kid as soon as he'd found the creature he sought. He remembered the homeless shelter he'd seen when they drove into town and nodded with satisfaction. *Soon, I can drop the brat there and move on.*

All he needed was a few more days, but he'd found him. *End of the line, Scourge of Transylvania. Your time is nigh.*

Viggo allowed an anticipatory grin to crease his lips as he bent to the computer to keep digging.

CHAPTER FIVE

A roughly cleared throat brought Aliandra back to the present from the lovely image of Drake's burning red eyes and lusty intensity.

Focus, focus, focus!

"All right, Mrs. McGillicutty, your heart rate and blood pressure are strong and normal, respectively, and your breathing is clear. How is your arthritis doing?" She pulled the stethoscope away from the old human's back and stood in front of her.

"Oh, it's okay as long as it doesn't snow."

Aliandra laughed because Mrs. McGillicutty expected her to. "Yes, well, we can hope, but I wouldn't hold my breath."

"That would only irritate my rheumatism." The old woman grimaced.

"Can't have that." Aliandra smiled. "Nothing else to tell me about?"

"Not unless I can get you to come over for Thanksgiving Dinner. My son Patrick is home from Yale." She smiled coyly. "He's studying to be a doctor, you know. You would have lots in common."

Goddess save me from match-making mamas.

"Thank you, Mrs. McGillicutty. That is a very kind invitation. But I'm on call this Thanksgiving so Dr. Keener can be with his family. I hear his daughter is coming into town."

Mrs. McGillicutty's burgeoning disappointment cleared into interest. "Would that be his single daughter?"

Aliandra hid her smile as she made some notes on the chart. "I don't believe Ms. Keener is married yet." She looked up and nodded. "Everything looks good with your health. I'll see you at your next check up. Have a good holiday and call me if your arthritis gets bad. We'll make sure you have enough glucosamine to see you through New Year's."

The old woman nodded absently and Aliandra took her leave. She suspected the crafty bird now plotted a way to get into Dr. Keener's Thanksgiving plans. Aliandra would be on call for the holiday, but she half wished she'd had plans to use as an excuse.

Plans with a tall, distinguished gentleman of the vampiric variety.

Drake's abrupt dismissal at the library had hurt more than she thought. She kept telling herself it didn't matter, that they hadn't shared anything too special in the clinic last night, but her heart kept ignoring her mind. Aliandra tightened her lips and tried to focus on the chart, writing her notes in a careful hand.

Finish the chart. Get back to work.

Aliandra dropped her pen and rubbed the muscles of her neck and shoulders, trying to massage away the memories of riding Drake's cock. Or how he'd blown her off that morning. Snarling, she rose to her feet and stomped out to leave the chart with Sally, their greeter.

She almost ran into someone, but he caught her before she collided with him. The scents of leather and ink-soaked parchment enveloped her as strong hands held her steady. She looked up into the glorious brown gaze of Drake

MacGregor and her pussy spasmed with need. She wanted to nestle her body against his and tease him into feeding from her again.

Hellwinds, I'm addicted.

"Careful, Dr. Cantora. Are you all right?"

Drake's sexy voice set her arousal blazing like a campfire and his eyes shot to crimson as his nostrils flared with her change in scent. Aliandra took a moment to settle herself into her professional façade and smiled, but the storm of arousal brewed beneath her surface. *You're not dealing with humans here. He can smell you. Calm down.*

"Yes, thank you. It was an early morning for me today." She straightened the chart and set it on the front counter before shoving her hands into her pockets to keep from touching him again. "What can I do for you, Mr. MacGregor?"

"Actually, I brought a visitor for you." Drake winked and stepped aside, revealing Tomarrion behind him.

"Hi, Aliandra. Is it okay to visit right now?"

Aliandra's smile broadened with real delight. "Hello, Tom. You're more than welcome."

"We can wait if you need more time to see patients. We just…" Drake trailed off as Tom nudged him. "*I* wanted to come by and apologize for my behavior at the library earlier today."

She raised her eyebrows.

Tom nudged him again. "Just say you're sorry. Girls like that."

"Thank you, Tom. I think I can take it from here," Drake whispered, winking at Aliandra. She clenched her jaws together to keep from grinning.

He stood tall and his expression softened. "Please forgive me, Dr. Cantora. I was short with you this morning because of the visitor in the Archives and I didn't want him—"

"To know about your personal business," she finished

for him.

"Yes. I tend to keep my private life…private."

"I understand, Mr. MacGregor."

He looked like he wanted to say more, but he only nodded and gave her a grimace. "Tom thought I should come by immediately and explain, and since he was invited here anyway, I thought I'd tag along." He winked again.

Flattery will get you everywhere. But she was inordinately pleased he'd made the effort and hoped she'd be able to speak with him more when they were alone.

"Well, that didn't take long." Aliandra smiled at both the man and the boy, and gestured toward her office. "I just happen to be in between patients at the moment. Why don't you gentlemen step into my office? I'll join you as soon as I finish this paperwork."

Drake nodded and took Tom's hand, leading him down the hallway. Aliandra couldn't help watching them walk away, her heart pounding with two conflicting emotions. Lust for the man and yearning for them both.

What is wrong with me? She ogled Drake's ass in his jeans below the hem of his coat. *Nothing's wrong in wanting that ass.*

But the yearning for a husband and son smacked her right between the eyes. And not just any husband and son, Drake and Tom. As a dragon, yearnings came and went, like the need to collect a hoard or visit the Ring of Fire to bathe in the earth's molten volcanic cauldrons. But to yearn for a mate and a family, Aliandra had never experienced that before.

Just sign the damn paperwork. She forced her focus back to the charts, signing quickly to get back to her family. *Guests! Hellwinds, they're only guests.*

Aliandra left the charts with the prescriptions for Mrs. McGillicutty for Angela to call in and almost ran down the hall to her office. The old woman's attempt at matchmaking Aliandra with her son Patrick reminded her she still didn't have any Thanksgiving plans.

Maybe I should ask what Drake and Tom are doing for the holiday.

She found the them in her office admiring her framed artwork. She'd collected them over the centuries from some of the great masters before they'd reached their greatness. Van Gogh's sailboats remained her favorite.

"Thank you for being so patient, gentlemen." She leaned against the desk. "I'm very glad to see you here. I was just speaking with Mrs. McGillicutty about the holidays."

Drake raised an eyebrow. "Is her son home for Thanksgiving?"

"Yes, she invited me to attend her family celebration."

Drake's jaw clenched, but he gave a tight smile. "I hear Patrick is doing well in his MD at Yale, and is still single. Much to his mother's dismay."

"She did say something to that effect." Aliandra shrugged. "But I'm on call that night and she lives too far out to reach the clinic quickly."

"You're going to be alone on Thanksgiving?"

"What's Thanksgiving?" Tom asked.

Aliandra thought it a strange question coming from a boy adopted by an American professor, but she shoved it aside. "It's an American holiday celebrating generosity, peace, and family on the last Thursday of November."

"Oh. I don't have any family." The sadness in Tom's voice squeezed her heart and she wanted to wrap her arms around him.

"What about Dr. Lance?" Drake squeezed Tom's shoulder.

"I don't think he celebrates anything."

Anger stirred at the hopelessness in the dragonet and she mustered up a cheery smile. "Well, then perhaps he'd let you join me for Thanksgiving at my home. You and Mr. MacGregor, both. What do you say?"

"I thought you're on call that night." Drake cocked his head.

"I am, but I don't live far and I can be here in a flash." She tried to still the sharp shot of fear he'd reject her invitation. "Would you join me for a Thanksgiving dinner?"

Drake exchanged a look with Tom and Aliandra held her breath. Why did she put herself out like this when she knew they could never have anything true? But she still hoped.

"We can't let her be alone on Thanksgiving." Drake spoke to Tom and the boy nodded gravely. They both turned to her and smiled. "We'd be delighted to share the holiday with you, Dr. Cantora. Can I bring anything to help in your feast?"

Relief and excitement cascaded through her and she grinned, her hands uncrimping from the edge of her desk. *Damn, I hope I didn't leave gouges.*

"Perhaps mashed potatoes? I'm terrible at them."

Drake laughed and arousal simmered just below the surface at the sound. "I haven't had much luck with them either, but I make a mean steamed asparagus and have been known to pick some very good rolls from the bakery."

Aliandra met his laugh with one of her own. "It's a date, then." She froze and flushed, wondering how she could be so forward. Her mother would be appalled, but she refused to take it back.

Before either of them could say more, the front desk buzzed to say her next patient had arrived.

"I should get back to the library and leave you to your patients." Mr. MacGregor extended his hand to her. "Again, please forgive me for my rudeness before, and I truly look forward to sharing Thanksgiving with you. What time would you like us to arrive?"

"Since I'm on call that evening, I thought we'd eat around two o'clock." She grasped his hand, allowing his heat to soak into her. "You're welcome to come earlier, if you'd like."

"Excellent." He brought her hand to his lips and she forced herself not to swoon from the light kiss against her knuckles. "I shall see you then."

He released her hand and she almost moaned with disappointment, but sealed her lips around the sound. No use making a fool out of herself too soon. She watched as Drake said goodbye to Tom, then strode out the door. Her heart tugged her after him, but she reminded herself she had another patient and assumed her game face.

"Come, Tom. Let's go have a look at Mr. Kirkland, shall we?"

****

Despite the mellowness of the mid-afternoon crowd in the library, Drake needed a quiet place to sit and think. With Aliandra's invitation to the Thanksgiving holiday the day before and Dr. Lance in his office, Drake's mind refused to settle. He retreated to the single study room they had in the little Three Lakes Library. He froze when he saw it occupied.

Damn. Now where?

Scanning the stacks around him, he found a single chair against a window that looked out on the little garden Bailey insisted was maintained by faeries. Drake snorted in amusement. She didn't know the dryads took pains to keep it up. Settling into the chair, he pulled out his tablet and tried to get to work.

If he wanted to spend more time with Aliandra—and his dick definitely wanted to—he'd need to make an effort to repair his standing within the Order of the Dragon. It had been two days since he'd taken her blood and only now had his feeding cravings started to intrude on his consciousness.

Human blood never satisfied me this long.

He grimaced, hoping his craving could be satisfied without the benefit of Aliandra's rich draconic blood. *Please, Goddess, promise me I'm not addicted already.* Not the best way to stay in her good graces if he was always jonesing for her blood.

Just read the texts.

Drake opened the files he'd been researching and took a deep breath. He read the texts and the prophecy. Then he read them again when his eyes caught on the word 'dragon'. His father had been the first knight in the Order of the Dragon and inducted Drake into it. According to the text in ancient Wallachian dialect, if someone should defile the Order, reparations must be made to the Order's founder, the Pope at the time.

Bloody hell, the founder has been dead longer than I have. How the hell am I going to make reparations?

He read the text again, this time slowly, puzzling out the meanings of each word. His blood ran colder than the streams feeding the Great Lake outside. He could make reparations to the founder or he could make a sacrifice to a dragon.

Drake's thoughts turned to Aliandra. What sort of sacrifice would she require?

He grimaced and shook his head, looking back down at the photograph of an ancient cross. The image called to mind dark, neglected sepulchers, and a place he was likely to visit if he pissed Aliandra off again. He knew he should apologize, but it might not be enough. How did one appease a dragon?

Closing the file, he rose and stretched, his mind turning over possibilities.

Start with flowers. As Tom would say, girls like that.

Drake almost laughed aloud, but the idea had merit and his shoulders relaxed for the first time since Dr. Lance and his "son" came into the library. From what the boy had told him, he'd stay with Aliandra whenever he could get away from Dr. Lance. While Drake really liked the boy, he hoped to have some personal time with Aliandra and try to make amends for his surly behavior.

"Bailey, I have to run some errands. I don't think I'll be back today."

"Everything okay, Mr. MacGregor?" Bailey looked up with concern crinkling her brow.

"Yes, just fine. But there are things I have to take care of and I don't expect to be back. See you tomorrow." He paused. "Be sure to tell Dr. Lance that his son is at the clinic and he can retrieve him there when the library closes."

"Okay. Have a good evening."

He collected his hat, scarf and coat, and dressed on the way out the door. The less time he spent in the library with Dr. Lance the better off everyone would be. The man made him surly.

The cold air hit his nostrils with snow and the songs of the Ice Demons in the wind. He loved to hear them singing and he suspected William Lutrenin, the local Selkie who'd married one, would be celebrating with his wife's visiting family on winter nights. The cold seared the stench from his office out of his nose and he strode through the swirling flakes with a smile curling his lips.

He pushed into the door of the Sweet Summer Blooms flower shop and reveled in the fragrances swirling within. Though winter howled outside, Karina Litton maintained summer existed somewhere on Earth, and so she always had flowers. This time of year her shop smelled mostly of orchids, cinnamon, cloves, and vanilla from the Thanksgiving arrangements she offered to the locals for the holiday.

"Good evening, Mr. MacGregor." Karina popped up from behind her counter with a big smile. "I haven't seen you in here in a while. How are things at the library?"

"Good, thank you."

"What brings you in today? Are you looking for something for your holiday celebration?"

He paused, wondering if he'd need something to help with the celebration at Aliandra's home, but shoved the thought aside. One conundrum at a time.

"No, I'm here for a more immediate reason. I need a bouquet of flowers."

Karina raised an eyebrow. "What kind of bouquet? An 'I'm sorry' bouquet or a 'get well soon' bouquet?"

Drake felt his face heat. "No, more of an 'I'm thinking of you' bouquet."

Karina's second eyebrow joined the first. "Well, this is a new development. What kind of flowers were you thinking? Is it serious enough for roses?"

Was it? He let his gaze slide around the shop, taking in the daisies, sunflowers, chrysanthemums, and marigolds. How did he express his heartfelt contrition without offending Aliandra? He didn't want her to think he apologized for the feeding and the sex. Though he still felt chagrin for that, he knew he'd insult her if he begged her pardon.

"Um, well, what do you give to someone you greatly esteem, and would like to see again, but may have offended accidentally?"

Karina raised an eyebrow. "That's a tall order, Mr. MacGregor. What kind of apology are you aiming for?"

"*Kind* of apology?"

"Yes, are you saying 'I'm sorry for being late or standing you up'? Or is it something more like 'Forgive me for being an arrogant ass'?"

"Uh..." How did he explain the disgrace he'd heaped upon the Order of the Dragon? While flowers wouldn't make full reparations, they'd definitely make Aliandra happy. At least, he hoped they would. "Maybe more of the latter?"

Karina nodded slowly. "Perhaps you could do a mix of

red and white roses."

"Roses? Don't they mean love?" His stomach did a little flip and landed hard.

"Red roses mean affection and fidelity, while white roses mean chastity, truth, and silence. If you've offended someone, usually by having an affair, this is a good way to show you're contrite."

"I haven't done that." The idea of cheating on Aliandra made him sick to his stomach. *Which won't happen because I'm not courting her.* "What would say 'I'm sorry for overstepping the bounds of friendship and please take my invitation to dinner seriously'?"

Karina looked at him a long time, long enough to make him want to squirm. "Intimate dinner?"

"Uh, well, just the two of us, yes."

"Definitely the red and white roses."

"Are you certain that won't suggest romance?"

"It's all in context, Mr. MacGregor." Karina opened a cooler and pulled out the largest rose buds he'd ever seen. Each one matched the size of his fist. "If you come to her with a proposal and this bouquet, she might think you wanted to marry her. If you come with the bouquet and an apology, I don't believe she'll think you want a life-long commitment."

He ignored the excited thump of his heart at the idea. "Very good, then."

"I'll just wrap them up for you. One dozen?"

"A baker's dozen, please. One extra for sincerity."

Karina smiled and prepared the bouquet, asking if he'd like a card. He shook his head and she added some baby's breath and tied everything together with a large green ribbon. Drake suspected this event would be news all over Three Lakes by morning, but it couldn't be helped. He had to make reparations to Aliandra.

And if he was lucky, she wouldn't burn him to a crisp when he apologized.

CHAPTER SIX

"What are these?"

Aliandra glanced up from the paperwork she'd just finished to the book in Tom's lap.

"People call them dragons."

Tom wrinkled his nose and shook his head. "That's not a dragon. Dragons are big and have wings and breathe fire."

"I know, but most humans don't believe in dragons, so they call lizards 'dragons.' I think that's a picture of a 'bearded dragon.'"

Tom shook his head and set the book aside, swinging his feet under his chair. "So why don't humans believe in dragons?"

"Because we don't want them to." Aliandra signed the last report and shoved it in the manila folder. "It's safer for everyone."

"Why?"

Aliandra wished Drake had come with them to the clinic. He was the historian. He could probably explain it better than she could, but he'd stayed at the library all day today. Dammit.

"Did your mom teach you much about the Elder Races

before she died?" Aliandra asked as she rose and dragged her doctor's stool over beside him.

"A little."

"Well, the dragons are the oldest of the Elder Races, Guardians of the world for the Goddess." Aliandra's heart warmed as she recited the tale for Tom. *Goddess, I so wish he was my son.* "Demons from the Underworld often found ways to get into Her world and caused havoc among the peoples She nurtured. The demons were particularly adept at damaging the humans because humans are predators and often react with violence to something they either fear or don't understand."

Tom considered her words, running his fingers over the raised title on the cover of the book. "Is that why we wear their costume? So we look like them?"

Aliandra smiled. "That's exactly why. We hide among them and protect them, but we can't tell them we're here because they'd be afraid of us."

"And try to hurt us."

"Yes."

"Like they hurt my parents."

"What?" Horror and surprise shot through Aliandra.

"My parents were killed by three men claiming they were warriors to god and my family needed to be destroyed," Tom whispered, his hands clenched on the book.

"Why?"

"I don't know. My mum threw me in the root cellar of our old shed and told me to stay there until the visitors went away." His face contorted with rage and grief. "I did as I was told. And now they're dead and I'm a coward."

Aliandra hugged him before her mind even registered the movement.

"Shh, shh, Tom, that's not true." She rocked him as he sobbed against her chest. "Your parents wanted to protect you. They knew something was very wrong and you were the most important thing to them. You weren't ready to fight for them yet and they knew that."

"But I didn't even try," he wailed.

"If you had, three dragons would've died that day." She rocked him gently. "Oh, *sa cherro*, it's not your fault and I'm grateful they didn't find you. I'm so glad you've come to Three Lakes and if you were my son, I'd do the same to protect you. Be at peace, *sa cherro*."

Aliandra held Tom until he released his grief. Her heart ached as she rocked him gently, offering what little solace she could. She looked for something to distract him and found the books lying open before her on the table.

"It looks like you were reading about airplanes again." She squeezed him a little. "Did you learn something new?"

Tom sniffed and nodded in her arms.

"What did you learn?"

He wiped his face. "I learned that most airplanes are either commercial or military. And there are a few most people didn't know about until long after they'd been decommissioned."

"You mean, spy planes."

"Yes." Tom sniffed and wiped his nose on his sleeve.

Aliandra nodded with a smug smile. "I was there when the first 'secret' one flew over my home in New Mexico. No one was supposed to know about it, but they made their practice flights at night and I saw them a few times from the air."

"You were flying the same time they were?" Tom knuckled his eyes.

Aliandra grinned and winked. "Yes. They never saw me above them." She leaned closer. "Apparently, dragons don't *ping* on their radar."

Tom giggled. "What's radar?"

"It's the use of radio waves to figure out the distance, altitude, direction and speed of motion of something flying in the sky. It's kind of like sonograms except that's using sound to figure out the size of something inside something else, like a baby in a mother. Would you like to see one?"

"Do you have a radar here?"

"No, but we have a sonogram. I can show you the machine, but until we have a patient that agrees, I can't show you what it can do."

"Would it work on tummies?"

Aliandra laughed. "Why? Is your tummy upset?"

"No, I just want to know if I can see it."

Aliandra looked at her watch. "Tell you what, I have an appointment with Mrs. Lindhurst in ten minutes for a checkup. She's pregnant. Maybe we can ask her if she'd let you see the sonogram at work then."

"All right. Thank you."

"You're welcome."

Tom gathered up some of the books into a neat pile then turned his gaze to the rows of medical books on the shelves of her office. "Aliandra, are you and Dr. Keener healers?"

She nodded. "As a matter of fact, we are. Why?"

"'Cause I wanna be one, too. Like you."

"What a sweet thing to say. Thank you. Let's just keep you as my assistant for now, okay?"

"Okay." Tom grinned and two dimples marked his cheeks.

Grateful joy filled Aliandra's heart and she couldn't stop the dopey smile curving her lips. *Oh Goddess, I wish I could have this little boy in my life.* He shouldn't have been left with a human, not after what humans had done to his family. Her stomach sank as a new thought occurred to her. *Hellwinds, Dr. Lance wasn't part of the men who killed Tom's family, was he?* She shoved the thought aside. *No way, Tom would've recognized him.*

Aliandra smiled back at him and wished she could watch him grow up. She wondered how he ended up with Dr. Lance, but Mrs. Lindhurst arrived and her question got pushed into the back of her mind. Mrs. Lindhurst was delighted to meet Tom and had no problem allowing him to watch the sonogram. Tom's curious questions and observations burrowed him deeper and deeper into Aliandra's heart.

"The heartbeat of the baby is very fast, almost twice as fast as an adult's at this stage."

She moved the hand-held over Mrs. Lindhurst's belly and snapped few digital photos of the baby for the chart. This kind of work soothed Aliandra. The simplicity of the baby developing in the mother's womb, the sound of the heartbeat, and the movements of the child made her focus on the present rather than her worries.

What she'd give to have one of her own.

Her gaze involuntarily strayed to Tom, and the pang in her heart deepened. He needed to be with dragons, not humans.

"All right, Mrs. Lindhurst. The moment of truth. Do you want to know the gender of the baby?"

The woman's eyes sparkled as she smiled. "Yes, please."

Aliandra roamed the head of the hand-held over Mrs. Lindhurst's belly, trying to find the best position to see the junction between the baby's legs. The baby chose to keep the legs together for the most part, but Aliandra coaxed it to move just enough to get a clear view.

"Congratulations, you're going to have a baby girl." Aliandra smiled. "Here's a good look at her face." She clicked a button on the keyboard to capture the delicate features in a printable photo.

"She's beautiful," Mrs. Lindhurst murmured, her eyes soft.

"Yes, she is."

Tom offered a brilliant smile. "When do we get to see her for real?"

"She'll be ready for her public debut in about four and

a half months." Aliandra snapped a few more pictures, then turned off the ultrasound and helped wipe the extra gel off the woman's abdomen. "Everything looks good. I'll see you in a month, Mrs. Lindhurst. Come along, Tom."

"That was amazing, Dr. Aliandra." He smiled as they walked down the hall to her office. "Is that the way it works with dragons, too?"

"What do you mean?" Aliandra shut her office door and sat at her desk. She didn't want to have this discussion in front of human ears.

"Do dragons develop in their mothers' bellies just like in humans?"

Aliandra frowned as she thought back. She knew a lot about human reproduction and medicine, but she hadn't paid attention to the same knowledge of draconic development. She'd never studied it because when her medical interest started, the culture of Peru didn't allow women to learn anything outside of being a mother, wife, or housekeeper. Aliandra had persevered by learning the more shamanic arts belonging to midwives and wise women until times allowed her to find more medical knowledge.

But it had all been associated with humans, not dragons.

"I believe they do, although it's not my area of expertise. We are warm blooded despite our reptilian origins, much like the theropod dinosaurs. But unlike them, we have had to hide our existence among the humans, and what better way to hide than to develop single, live births? Instead of eggs, dragons now give birth, in either form, to live offspring, one at a time I believe."

"Someone should write a book about it, so we can learn more about dragons." Tom gave her an earnest look.

"I can't say anyone *hasn't* written one, I just haven't read one. I think it would be quite dangerous for dragons if the humans got a hold of such knowledge, though." Tom looked crestfallen and a haunted look crossed his face. Aliandra cursed her insensitivity. The deaths of his parents still resonated with him. "Tell you what, maybe at Thanksgiving we'll start our own dragon book. You can help me write down our observations of what it's like to be a dragon. We'll keep it at my house so it's just for us. What do you think?"

He nodded slowly. "Okay, Aliandra."

The clock in her office gave an hourly chime and she blinked when she realized how late it had gotten. "Let me finish this paperwork then I'll take you back to the library and Dr. Lance."

Neither of them ever mentioned the doctor as his father. Tom didn't say anything, but he withdrew into himself the closer the time came to leave. Aliandra hated to see his exuberance and joy of life so curtailed, but he wasn't her responsibility, as much as she'd like him to be.

They bundled up and headed out into the frigid windy evening, Tom becoming quieter and quieter as they approached the library. She wished she could pull him away from the man claiming to be his adopted father, but until she had a legitimate cause, she could do nothing.

He's a dragon with a human. Surely that's legitimate cause enough? Except it would expose them both to human awareness and she couldn't endanger either of them that way. *Hellwinds.*

They entered the library and found the Archives empty except for Dr. Lance. The smell had gotten worse and not even Bailey's sweet-scented pine boughs could cover it up. Aliandra looked for Drake, but his desk sat empty and his laptop remained closed. She tried to quell the surge of disappointment.

"Thank you for the lovely day, Dr. Cantora." Tom gravely shook her hand as Dr. Lance laid a hand on Tom's shoulder. The boy shivered a little, but his expression didn't change. "I learned a lot today. May I please come back tomorrow?" He begged her with his eyes even while his face remained serene.

"That would be fine with me, but you will have to check with Dr. Lance." Truth be told, Aliandra wanted Tom away from the odious man as much as possible.

"That is all right as long as you mind your manners and stay out of the doctor's way." Lance leveled a stern look Tom's way.

"Yes, sir." Tom bobbed his head in agreement.

"Very well. I'll allow Thomas to visit. If, at any time, he becomes a bother, please let me know and we'll make other arrangements." Dr. Lance gave her a charming smile.

The words and the smile should have put Aliandra at ease, but the stench wafting off him gave him an air of malignancy she couldn't shake. She didn't allow him to shake her hand.

"Good. I'll see you tomorrow morning at eight o'clock sharp, Tom."

"Okay, Dr. Cantora."

She nodded to them both and retreated from the library, desperate to get out into the clean air. She inhaled great gulps, trying to rid herself of the stench clogging her nose. Why did that man stink so badly? She shook her head and strode for home, sudden sympathy for Drake flooding her mind. His sense of smell rivaled her own and she couldn't stand to be in the same building with Dr. Lance, much less in the same room.

How does he do it?

Aliandra allowed the pleasing image of Drake to push aside the heinous Dr. Lance from her mind. *His* features filled her with a sense of belonging and warmth. He smelled divine, even though his main nourishment came from blood. She'd expected vampires to smell of dried plasma, the grave, and death, but Drake's scent made her mouth water right along with her pussy.

She sighed as arousal flickered with her thoughts, her

breath pluming out in front of her as she reached her porch. She wanted to see him again and try to coax more of his smiles. When he smiled his rich brown eyes sparkled like molten chocolate, and she loved the bitter sauce made from the cacao beans. Hellwinds, she'd offer him more of her blood just to feel his hands on her again.

Deep breaths there, Cantora. He might not want more of my blood. She ignored the urge to flaunt it in front of him like a bullfighter's cape as she pushed open her front door.

Aliandra started the fire in the fireplace to warm up her house as her thoughts turned to the invitation she extended to the two males she liked most in this town. Her heart sped up at the thought of celebrating with Drake and Tom. Her own little family.

Stop those thoughts right now. Neither of them are my family.

But she wanted them to be.

"Focus on dinner."

She rose and headed toward the kitchen, but a knock at her door made her divert her course. Her nose filled with the succulent scent of roses before she'd even opened the door, but the sight of huge red and white blooms against the graying world beyond her porch warmed her heart better than fire. Even more welcome than the roses, Drake's face appeared behind the large bouquet, and her lips creased into a delighted smile.

"Mr. MacGregor?"

"Good evening, Dr. Cantora. May I come in for a moment?"

"Oh, of course. Come in out of the cold." She backed inside and held the door open, the heat blooming through her banishing any cold he brought in with him. "What brings you by my home?"

A lopsided smile full of mild chagrin and boyish charm crossed his face. "I wanted to come and truly apologize for my brusqueness over the last few days. I know I visited your office and you kindly invited me to Thanksgiving, but I wanted to make sure you know I meant it." He extended the bouquet. "These are for you."

She took the roses and inhaled, reminding herself roses didn't necessarily mean love or fidelity. *It's a sweet gesture and one I will encourage.*

"Thank you so much. They weren't necessary, but I love them."

His shoulders relaxed as if he'd been worried she wouldn't accept them. "I also wanted to invite you to have dinner with me, um, sometime."

"Tonight?" She cursed as he backpedaled, his expression changing to uncertainty.

"Well, no, not if you're too busy. I don't want to impose on your free time."

"No, no. I was just thinking I didn't know what I'd be having for dinner, and if you're not busy tonight, it would be a welcome change in plans." *Please, please say yes.*

Damn, she sounded like an over-eager teen-aged girl. At nearly eleven hundred years old, she should know better. *Pull yourself together…but Goddess, please let him accept.*

Drake's smile returned. "Excellent. Would you care to go out or stay in?"

Lurid thoughts of staying in bed with Drake while he sucked her blood from various places on her body filled her mind. Her pussy clenched with delighted need and she swallowed hard around her smile. Staying in might not be a good idea.

Or it might be the best idea.

Three Lakes was a small town and with it came small town gossip. Aliandra didn't relish sharing Drake with anyone else just yet. She preferred to keep her interest in him private for a little while longer.

"Well, I just started a fire in the fireplace and I have

some shark steaks in the fridge. I might be able to find some wine to go with it."

"You have shark steaks?"

Drake unzipped his jacket and unwound his scarf from around his neck. Her gaze fixed on the column of his throat and her lips dried out so fast, she had to lick them. She wanted to bite him there so hard, sink her fangs into the muscle of his shoulder until her jaws ached as she rocked on his stiff cock.

Drake froze, his gaze locked on her face. Some emotion flashed through his expression too fast for her to identify, but his cheeks flushed and he swallowed hard.

"Are you well, Doctor?"

"Yes, I'm fine." She blinked a few times, coming back to herself. "Let me put these in water before they wilt."

She turned on her heel and forced herself to walk into her kitchen. *Focus, focus, focus.* She heard him behind her, but refused to look until she'd filled a vase with water for the roses. Each one smelled wonderful, but the rose scents only complimented the spicy male who joined her in the kitchen. Her skin tingled with awareness and her pussy ached with the need to feel his cock again.

"There." She turned to display the roses and stopped when she caught sight of his expression. His eyes glittered in the low light of the under-cabinet lamps and he looked hungry, but not for food. Her nipples tightened inside her sweater and she resisted the urge to rub them to relieve the hard ache. "Is anything wrong, Mr. MacGregor?"

It was his turn to blink and shake himself to awareness. "Oh, uh, no. No. The roses look better in your kitchen than I imagined." He lifted his arm filled with coat and rubbed the back of his neck.

"Oh, here, let me take your coat." Aliandra set the roses down on the dining room table and reached for the fabric. When he handed it to her, their hands brushed and an electric tingle raced up her arm. She gasped and more cream flooded between her pussy lips. Why had she become so hyperaware of him?

She met his gaze and he stared back at her with hot desire filling his face. His jaw clenched and she wanted to kiss it until it relaxed. She'd be happy just resting against his chest, inhaling his delicious scent. *With my hands thrust down his shorts.*

Aliandra came back to herself standing nearly nose to nose with him, her hands braced on his arms. *When did I move here?* She cleared her throat and stepped back.

"I'm sorry, Mr. MacGregor. I seem to be having trouble focusing on propriety."

"It's all right, Doctor. I, uh, am having a similar difficulty." He stared down at her with intensity burning beneath his irises and heat bloomed across her cheeks. "Given our previous associations, though, perhaps you'd do me the honor of calling me Drake."

"Drake."

A visible shiver rocked his body and she wanted to wrap her own body around him to provide comfort. The scents of warmed leather and spicy chocolate hit her nose and she inhaled deeply as she closed her eyes. His breathing increased along with the heat of his body as his hands cupped her face.

Before she could say a word, his lips sealed on hers.

Fire and lust burned a brilliant trail through her body and her nipples hardened enough to hurt. She threw her body against his to relieve the ache, dropping his coat. He growled and caught her, his tongue lashing her own inside her mouth as they tumbled to the floor.

Drake rolled over on top of her and pressed his hips against hers, grinding a solid ridge of wool-covered flesh against her mound. Delicious shots of pleasure hit her clit with each slide of his hard cock through their clothes and she moaned, rocking her own hips.

Their tongues dueled for erotic supremacy as she dug

her fingers into his shoulders and he drew back with a hiss. Blazing eyes of red looked down at her, hunger flushing his cheeks a rosy color. His lips pulled back from his teeth and his elongated canines flashed, sending arousal straight to her pussy.

Goddess, I want him to bite me.

"Drake," she whispered. "Bite me."

As if a bucket of ice water had been thrown over them, Drake froze and the red retreated from his eyes. All the color faded from his cheeks as his expression turned to chagrin and his canines retreated back to human length.

"Sweet Goddess, I'm so sorry, Dr. Cantora. I...I don't know what came over me..."

Drake started to pull away, but she locked her arms around him to hold him still. "Wait."

"If you want, you can get up now, Doctor. I won't hold you here."

She almost laughed since she held him down. "Aliandra."

"What?"

"The name is Aliandra, and what if I don't want to get up yet?"

He blinked, the thoughts churning behind his eyes as she reached up with one had to stroke his face. "What if I would rather you feed from me again as you make love with me?" She rubbed her thumb against the corner of his mouth, lifting his lip to show one canine.

"No." He closed his eyes and shook his head hard. "No, I came here to apologize to you. To make up for my past transgressions. Not to feed from you again, to dishonor you again."

"What? How could you dishonor me by feeding from me?"

"Because...you're a dragon. Dragons are to be revered and held sacred. They shouldn't be used as food." His jaw clenched.

Aliandra smirked, trying to break his resistance. "Well, that's true." She chuckled as he raised his brows. "But what if I request it because it brings me pleasure?"

Drake looked at her for a long moment. "It brings you pleasure?

She shivered. "Oh, yes." Aliandra wriggled beneath him, grinding her mound against his rigid cock. "So much pleasure."

He groaned as his shaft flexed and sent delicious swirls of excitement through her. "You are a temptation I should resist."

"I don't know about that. I think you should give in." She wriggled again.

"Oh, Goddesss." Drake sighed and swallowed hard. "Let's just start with dinner and go from there, all right?"

"What kind of dinner are we talking here?" Aliandra widened her smirk. "Blood is your main form of nourishment, correct?"

"Aliandra, please."

At least he'd gotten her name right. "Oh, all right." She wriggled once more, this time to get out from under him, but he held her down with his own smirk. "Are you going to let me up?"

"Yes, but only after one more kiss."

Aliandra blinked at him. "I thought I was a temptation you should resist."

"You are, but I'm a glutton for punishment and I want more of your sweet torture." Drake dropped his head and captured her mouth, sliding his tongue between her lips. Her arousal exploded as her pussy spasmed with desire and she whimpered. She found the tips of his canines and stroked, pulling a desperate groan from him, but he pulled back.

"Okay. Now dinner." He used the table to get up.

Aliandra whined, but allowed him to tug her to her feet. "Are you sure you don't need a snack before we eat?"

He chuckled and gave her a dark look. "Don't push me, Aliandra. I don't think 'snack' would accurately describe what I want to do."

The power and sexual eroticism in his voice sent cream rushing to her panties, but she merely bit her bottom lip and tried to remember what she'd been planning to make for dinner. *We were talking about...shark steaks. That's right.*

She skirted around him back to the kitchen, her skin still begging for more of his touch. Aliandra tried to think of something else. *Shark steaks, olive oil, garlic, salt...* Each ingredient appeared as if by magic as her thoughts fluttered like little birds. *Focus!*

"So shark steaks will be okay?" She knew the question was dumb the moment it left her mouth, but tried to smile anyway.

"They'll be fine, thank you. Is there anything I can help with?" Drake leaned against the doorway to the kitchen.

Just the sight of him in her home made her mouth water. She jerked her gaze away from him before her nipples peaked again. Her gaze landed on the vase full of roses on the table and some of her arousal drained away.

"I thought we'd have some fresh green beans with garlic butter glaze. Did you really bring the roses to apologize?"

Drake blinked at the change in subject. "Yes, Karina at the flower shop said they represented affection and truth, to show contrition. I regretted attacking you at the clinic the other night, as well as being short with you at the library."

I'm just crazy enough to enjoy being attacked.
"They're very sweet. Thank you. Apology accepted."

Drake's shoulders relaxed and he smiled. "Thank you. And you're welcome."

"Now, just keep me company while I cook. Would you like some wine?" *Dragon blood wine in particular?* She tried to smile despite her lusty thoughts.

"Best to keep my wits about me. Hot tea would be nice, though."

Aliandra shrugged away her sense of disappointment and set the kettle on to boil. *Take your time. Remember what it's like to go hunting.* She turned her attention to preparing the meal, but she couldn't help swinging her hips a bit more than necessary as she walked, or brushing his body with hers when she passed by.

A few times, Drake inhaled as if tempted to do more than watch, but he managed to hold onto his control. *I'll just have to try harder.*

"Did you hear Bruce and Gemini are having an engagement party next weekend?"

"Wait, Bruce the Sheriff is getting married to Gemini?"

"Yes. She asked him over the weekend and he accepted her suit." Aliandra smiled as she seasoned the shark steaks. "I think it's rather romantic."

"Isn't he a dwarf giant and she a fairy?" Drake frowned. "Rather odd pairing."

She paused, scanning his face. "Are you opposed to interspecies relationships?"

What if he said yes? What if part of his avoidance was because of her species?

"No, but it'll be harder to have children."

"Not everyone wants children, Drake." *Even if I do.* "And there's nothing wrong with not having any. A woman's value isn't in the offspring she produces." Aliandra ignored the disappointed looks her mother wore every time she went home.

"Of course not. But family is important." Drake's expression spoke of old pain, but he met her gaze and gave her a forced smile. "And not all extended families handle differences well. Both Bruce's and Gemini's families are rather traditional."

"Yes, but I think that's part of what they have in

common. And they could always adopt. Plenty of children out there who need loving parents."

Aliandra contemplated the idea as the green beans steamed. *Maybe I should consider adoption. I'm successful and family-oriented.* But honestly she didn't want just any child. She wanted one who understood her bloodline and species. And she wanted a lover or husband to share the parenting duties. She'd seen enough single mothers trying to make it and the world remained unkind to them. It angered her to see the lack of compassion leveled at women who tried despite overwhelming odds.

But she wanted a family, and if strictly honest, she wanted her family to be made up of Drake MacGregor and Tom Lance. Her mother would be appalled, but maybe not if she brought the dragonet home with her.

"Are you well, Aliandra?"

Drake's voice permeated her reverie and she came back to the scents of garlic and butter, and a sexy vampire male standing at her side.

"What? Oh, yes, I'm sorry." She hissed a little as she removed the shark steaks from the heat. "I didn't mean to drift off. Just thinking about family."

"Yours?" He took the beans from her and scraped them into a bowl she'd set out.

"Yes, and the one I'd like to have." She gave him a dismissive smile. "Dragons live a long time and it's hard when we choose paths so different from our brethren. I like humans, for the most part, and I like learning about them. My family thinks I'm insane and should use my healing abilities on our people rather than the world at large."

"You really prefer being with other species?" Drake helped her set out the food on her little kitchen table.

I really prefer being with you.

"Yes." She lit a couple of candles to give it a festive air. "Dragons become insular and forget our original purpose for being here."

"Which is?" Drake sat in one of the chairs as she set their plates filled with steaming steaks on the table.

"To protect all the Goddess's children from demons, even the demons that come from within their ranks." Aliandra settled across the table from him, enjoying the way the light caressed the planes of his face. "Hard to do that if we stay away from everyone."

"But it adds to your mystique if you do."

She raised an eyebrow at him and he winked, making her laugh as she served the beans. "I think I'd rather have gratitude than mystique. Awfully lonely being mysterious."

Drake lost his smile and his shoulders drooped. "Yes, I understand that very well."

Sorrow leaked across the table and Aliandra reached out to grasp his hand before she realized she'd moved. Instant recognition flared through the simple touch. *True Mate here.* Drake raised his gaze and met hers, his eyes widening with the same surprise zinging through her. What startled her most was the overwhelming urge to gather him into her arms and hold his sorrow at bay.

Drawing him out seemed like a better plan. "Do you? I'd think being the librarian of a small northern Michigan town would be pretty straight-forward."

"I meant about the loneliness." Drake dropped her gaze and dug into his food.

"How long have you been alone? Did you never have a wife or partner?" *Holy Goddess, maybe he's married.* Aliandra swallowed hard around a large chunk of steak and tried not to choke. *He's not wearing a ring on either hand...*

"Too long. My wife died..." He shook his head. "I shouldn't be talking about her while I'm with you. It's been centuries." He cleared his throat and gave her a half-smile. "I moved here about a hundred and fifty years ago when they were just starting the library. And with what I know, I was the logical choice for head librarian. I've been here ever since."

"But no other wife or girlfriend in all that time?"

Drake snorted. "I'm a bit too old to have a girlfriend."

"I don't know." Aliandra winked. "Lots of cute young things like older, distinguished men."

"I think it's the sanguineous diet that would turn them off." He shrugged. "It just seemed easier to live on my own and keep the records accurate."

She nodded. "Sounds like something a dragon would do, too." She paused to watch him as they ate in silence for a few moments. "But it seems to me like you're hiding from something."

"What?" His chocolate brown eyes met hers with surprise.

She shrugged to dispel some of his unease. "I just get the impression you're here to lay low or to punish yourself for something."

He swallowed hard and drank some of the wine from his glass, gulping it down like water. "Why would you think that?"

She shrugged again. "Maybe because whenever you get close to me or act on our connection, you run and hide for days afterwards."

CHAPTER SEVEN

Drake resisted the urge to bolt out of Aliandra's home.
Two things wrong with doing that. First, it was supremely
rude, and second, she was likely faster than him, even in
her human form. But he couldn't tell her about his
shortcomings. Not yet.

He tried to cover his unease with a short laugh. "Yes,
well, I've been out of the dating scene for centuries now
and haven't quite gotten the hang of these modern times
yet."

Aliandra snorted. "This is you "not getting the hang"
of the dating scene? Did panic work back when you were a
young man?"

He grimaced. "No, not then, either."

She sighed and set her empty plate aside. "Look,
Drake. I get it. You're a vampire and I'm a dragon. I don't
know what your past was like, but we're not in your past.
We're here, now, and we're both adults. What's the
problem?"

"But should we be dating? Especially because I'm a
vampire and you're a dragon."

"Is that what we're doing? Dating?" She snorted and
shook her head. "Call me old fashioned, but having a guy

have sex with me once and avoid me from then on doesn't count as dating in my mind."

Chagrin ate at him from the inside. He'd come to her house to apologize, but now he'd gotten fangs-deep in uncharted waters and had lost track of what he'd intended. And sharing that kiss before dinner hadn't helped his concentration.

Drake cleared his throat. "Perhaps this wasn't such a good idea."

"What wasn't?"

"Coming here tonight to apologize." He wiped his mouth on his napkin and gathered himself to get up. "I should probably go—"

"Sit." Her voice hadn't risen, but the sharp order solidified him to his chair.

He raised his gaze to meet her peacock-green eyes and swallowed hard at the anger and lust swirling there. "You want to make it up to me, Drake? Stop apologizing for something I liked. Stop regretting. Life is far too long to wallow in regret. Do you want to know how you can make it up to me?"

He swallowed hard at the fire in her gaze. "How?"

"Feed from me and make love with me."

"What?"

"What part didn't you understand?"

"You want me to…to feed from you? Again?" Lust and desire warred with shame and guilt from her request.

"Yes." Aliandra raised her chin. "You said you wanted to make it up to me."

"But by doing the same thing I apologized for?" Drake couldn't believe he argued with her when his heart screamed for him to take her up on the offer.

Aliandra stared at him for several heartbeats and he felt the opportunity slipping away as she sighed. "Fine. Thank you for the flowers and for sharing dinner with me."

Oh, Goddess, she's dismissing me. He frantically

searched his mind for something to say to fix the mess he'd made. "Shall I help you clean up?"

She shook her head and stood, taking her half-eaten dinner to the kitchen. He cursed under his breath and grabbed his own plate, thinking fast. Did he want to leave and head back to his cold apartment? *Hell no.* He preferred to be with Aliandra. *So fix it, numbskull.*

"Aliandra." He brought the plate to the kitchen, ignoring the idea he poked the dragon. *Even if I am.* "I'm—" She shot him a withering glance and he cut himself off. "I'm trying to understand so I'm clear on what you want. Because the desire and lust pounding in my skull is making it hard to think."

Not the most elegant or romantic way of saying it, but Aliandra's lips creased into a smile and the fire in her eyes reignited. She took his plate and set it aside before pulling him close by his lapels. He towered over her by a good eight inches, but she could easily rip him in half if she chose. Right now, if he resisted, she could tear his clothes off his body. *That's an idea.*

"So you desire to feed from and make love with me, Drake?"

"More than I've wanted to from anyone ever before." Truth rang in his voice as much as through his gut. He'd wanted Aliandra for years, but his secrets and his guilt held him back until now. Her offer had caught him off-guard, but the lure of her charms proved too tempting to resist.

"Good. As long as we're clear." She pushed up on her toes and brushed her lips over his.

Lust and yearning blasted through him, taking much of his control. He moaned and leaned in closer, tasting her lips. Flavors of the meal they'd eaten and her own spicy chocolate mixed as she thrust her tongue into his mouth, and his cock swelled in arousal. *Damn, this woman isn't shy about what she wants.* The revelation came with a dose of pleasure so strong, he growled.

She growled back at him and wrapped her arms around his back, pulling him so close her breasts flattened against his chest. Her peaked nipples dug through his clothes and his cock flexed in appreciation. He needed to taste her, touch her. *Feed on her enriched blood.* The desire for her rich elixir of life only surged when his mind inserted the image of feeding while fucking her sweet, hot pussy.

Drake had experienced sex hundreds of times over his lifespan, but no one had ever compared to the glorious heat of being inside Aliandra. She gave a whole new meaning to the word "hot". He tangled his fingers in her glorious black satin tresses and tugged her head back to deepen their kiss.

When he pulled back to meet her iridescent green gaze, he drowned in the passion suffusing her expression. She raised her chin and smirked, challenging him to either continue or run. *Though, Goddess knows, if I run, she'll catch me with her big claws.* The idea had merit, but he squashed the mischievous notion.

"Perhaps you'd be more comfortable in the bedroom?" He had no idea where the presence of mind came from, but she rumbled a laugh and took one of his hands.

"Come with me, *sa kierna*."

"What does that mean?" Drake followed Aliandra through her living room and down a short hallway decorated with dried flowers in frames with handwritten notes beside them.

"It's an endearment in my people's language. It means 'my soul.'" She gave him a sultry smile.

Heat burned throughout his chest and the blood shot straight to his cock. "You think of me as your soul?"

"Definitely a large piece of it."

She pulled him into a bedroom filled with jewel-tones. A patchwork quilt made from velvets and silks covered the bed. More framed dried flowers hung on the walls, some exotic varieties not seen in North America. The room had an overall hexagonal shape and smelled of mesquite wood, much like Aliandra herself.

"Clothes off. Now." She tugged at his sport coat and he grinned as he shrugged out of it.

"Yes, Doc."

Her eyes glowed a feral iridescent green and she stood back as he reached for his fly. His cock flexed with arousal as he took in her intense expression. She watched his every move, an anticipatory smile curling her lips.

"Is this what you wanted, Aliandra?"

"Oh, yes, Drake." She sauntered up to him as he freed his cock and it brushed against her belly. "You have no idea how badly I've wanted you." She wrapped one small, hot palm around his shaft and squeezed gently. "This is your chance to undo what's been done, and make love with me."

"Undo what's been done?" He had trouble thinking around the grip she had on his cock.

"Yes, all the running and avoiding and apologizing." She tugged in time with each word and he groaned. "Make love with me, feed from me, and all your past actions will be forgiven."

A small logical voice tried to insert a warning about dishonoring the Order of the Dragon with a real dragon, but he was done listening to his conscience tonight. He'd wanted and yearned for Aliandra, and she offered salvation in her arms. *By the Goddess, I'm taking this tonight.*

"Now, lie on the bed." Aliandra released his cock and pointed behind him. "I want to look at you there and remember it forever."

He backed away, never taking his gaze from hers. His cock swayed with his movements, but the tug of its engorged weight only turned him on more. He crawled backwards onto the bed and lay against the pillows. Aliandra licked her lips and his cock flexed in appreciation.

"Perfect." Aliandra pulled her sweater over her head and unzipped her slacks. She tossed the sweater over a plush chair and pushed her pants down her thighs.

Drake's mouth watered as his gaze fixed on her taut and supple legs. She hadn't worn any underwear and he groaned. *Sweet Goddess, she's been walking around commando.* His cock flexed again and he fisted the bedding to keep from launching at her.

When she unhooked her bra, he clenched his teeth at the sight of her hard, dusky nipples begging him to suckle them. The scent of her arousal perfumed the air and he took a deep, appreciative breath. She cocked one hip to the side and gave him a sultry smile.

"Like what you see, Drake?"

"Oh, Goddess, yes."

Aliandra chuckled deep in her throat and it rattled to his core. "See what you've been missing this whole time you avoided me? There's no reason to keep denying yourself."

Again, the warning voice in the back of his head spoke up, but he slapped it quiet and locked it in a box.

"I'm not denying myself the pleasure of your body tonight, Aliandra."

Her grin widened. "Excellent news."

She paused at the foot of the bed and unabashedly admired his naked body, her eyes glowing with arousal and need. Drake returned the favor, studying her lithe form with the dark nipples topping full breasts and the trimmed triangle of dark curls at the juncture of her thighs.

"You're so beautiful." He shifted to sit up, but she hissed and shook her head.

"You will stay put until I've had my fill, *sa kierna.*" She crawled onto the bed like a predator and licked her lips. "And right now, I plan to gorge myself on hot vampire cock."

She pushed his legs apart and lay down on her stomach between them, never taking her gaze from his flexing shaft. His balls tightened with delicious anticipation and he swallowed a whimper as she brushed his inner thighs. *Oh, sweet Goddess, yes.*

"I'm going to suck on your cock, Drake, until you come so hard you forget your own name."

Her voice had grown low and rough like raw silk, and he shivered with delight. He gasped as she wrapped her hand around his straining shaft and fitted her lips over the head. He moaned and dug his fingers into the bedcovers.

He stared down his body at her as she used her tongue to probe the slit, a smile curling the corners of her mouth. When she slid her mouth all the way down his shaft, he couldn't hold back his whimper. Hot, wet pressure engulfed his cock and his eyes rolled back in his head from the pleasure.

Aliandra growled around his shaft and the vibrations elicited his own growl. "Holy Goddess, that feels so damn good."

She pulled her head off his cock and licked her lips. "I couldn't agree more." She grinned and he shivered at the sight of her elongated canines. Something about the idea of those long teeth sliding against his cock had him moaning in anticipation.

She dipped her head and surrounded his cock with her scorching mouth. The sensation of those long teeth on his skin had him whimpering. She tightened her lips and licked the edges of the head. Drake swore his own canines would snap off he clenched his jaws so tight. Instead, his hands fisted the bedclothes and he hoped he wouldn't tear them.

The heat from her mouth combined with the suction and his balls tightened up against the base of his cock. The pleasure built so high his brain seemed to float. Drake closed his eyes and held on, wondering how he'd managed to go so long without Aliandra's touches.

Stupid fool.

"Oh Goddess, suck me hard, Aliandra. Yes, yessssss."

The pleasure boiled up, flooding through his mind until

he was swept away with it as she rumbled around his cock in approval. His release started at his spine and shot into her hot mouth as he roared. Pleasure threw him out into the cosmos and he lost track of the world. Stars flashed behind his closed lids and he sailed among them with joy. He'd never come so hard in his long life and the orgasm left him spent, but hungry for more.

Aliandra grinned around his cock as she licked the last of his release from his skin. "You're tasty, Drake."

He laughed breathlessly. "I strive to please, my dragon lady."

"Oh, that's very good news." She grinned as she crawled up his body until she straddled his hips. His cock flexed and slowly stiffened as he caught the scent of her increased arousal. Hot chocolate mixed with the fragrant spice of mesquite wood filled his nose and his cock stiffened more.

"You're magnificent, Aliandra." He wanted her more than he wanted his next breath. He wanted to love her, feed from her, and give her immeasurable pleasure.

"Thank you for the compliments."

"I have many more to give if you'd only let me offer them."

"Then I shall take them all, along with this." She grasped his hard shaft and sank down onto it, and Drake fell into a searing abyss of glory.

He sat up and grasped her hips as she wrapped her arms around his shoulders. She met his gaze as she rocked slowly on his cock, biting her bottom lip with a sultry smirk. He growled and slanted his lips over hers, thrusting his tongue into her mouth. Sweet, chocolaty heat hit his taste buds and he had to have more. His cock swelled inside her tight channel and the pleasure threatened to take him for another ride.

She matched his thrusts, riding him with ever tightening spasms of her pussy on his shaft. Her eyes blazed with lust and delight, and she moaned as he rocked his hips harder. Her inner muscles clamped down on his cock, rippling over it with delicious friction. Need, desire, and a possessiveness alien to him rose in his chest as he peppered her checks and neck with nipping kisses.

"I'm going to take you, Drake, and ride you hard." Aliandra's voice had grown guttural and she ground her hips against his. "I want you. You're mine, sweet vampire. Mine like the best jewels found in the walls of the Andes." She dug her fingers into his shoulders and grinned as she bore down on him. "I will keep you, treasure you, and love you forever."

Drake had never been beta to anyone before, but Aliandra's possessive words ramped up his arousal and made him want to expose his neck to her canines. Intellectually, he knew the urge came from his vampiric heritage. When meeting their true mates, vampires would bond with their partner by allowing them to drink from their veins. *But she's a dragon.* The protest was lost in a flood of lust as his balls tightened in warning to his impending orgasm.

"You're mine, *sa kierna.*" Aliandra snarled, baring her teeth in a lustful grin. Her body rocked harder, squeezing his cock in delicious power. "Mine forever. Mine, mine, mine..." Her voice rose and she threw her head back as her pussy clamped down hard on his cock.

Drake's release ignited as his cock swelled into granite-like hardness, and he clamped his hands on her hips as he watched her fly. His own ecstasy shot out of his balls, surging from his cock to fill her hot depths.

Their cries of pleasure filled the room in a perfect harmony as Drake lost himself to the joy. Ecstasy burned bright paths in his awareness and he would've floated there in her tight embrace if the sensation of teeth in his shoulder hadn't seared through the bliss. He gasped and shot into an even higher surge of pleasure, yanking his eyes open.

Aliandra growled at his neck, her teeth sunk into the muscle of his shoulder and his pleasure expanded until he couldn't hold back the urge to bite. He twisted around and sank his own fangs into her jugular. The richness of her blood made him swoon, and his orgasm pushed him higher. Aliandra moaned around his shoulder and Drake swallowed her glorious blood in three great gulps, before his sated mind allowed him to release her and lick her wounds closed.

They slowly came down together, and she pulled back to rest her forehead against his wounded shoulder. Despite the bite mark, he didn't feel any pain. Instead, he felt the greatest satisfaction of his life, as if he'd come home to the right place and right woman. *Mine.*

****

Aliandra sat with her head against Drake's shoulder and her pussy full of thick, hard vampire cock. Spectacular rainbows of pleasure and satisfaction unlike she'd ever experienced filled the space behind her closed eyelids. *This is what Mother meant by True Mating.* She rested in the ecstasy for a few moments, breathing in the scents of their sexual pleasure and the sounds of his breathing beside her.

Drake MacGregor is my True Mate. The idea was both frightening and exhilarating. How she could be True Mated to a vampire defied logic, but she didn't feel very logical at the moment. *Fucking fantastic, but not logical.* She inhaled deeply and a small prick of pain at her neck reminded her he'd bitten her as well. *And fed.* She shivered with the remembered pleasure and raised her head.

Drake still held her hips with his hands, his chest rising and falling with his slowing breaths. His skin glowed a healthy pink from the infusion of blood he'd taken and his hair draped into his face in long tendrils. She reached up to push it aside and he opened his eyes.

"Hello there, *sa kierna.*" She smiled, so grateful to have him in her bed. *He's mine now. We're mated.* The thrill of finding such a divine connection warmed her.

His cock flexed within her pussy as a smile curled his lips. "Hello, my beautiful, sexy dragon lady."

"I've missed you." She hadn't meant to admit it, but the night he'd fed from her in the clinic weighed on her memory and her soul yearned for more.

"Missed me?" His brows lowered, but the smile remained. "How have you missed me?"

"I've missed more of this." She waved at where they sat still joined. "Since that night in the clinic, I've wanted more with you." She ducked her head to rest it on his shoulder, suddenly shy. "I love you, Drake."

His sharp intake of breath told her she'd surprised him, but his arms tightened around her and he kissed the side of her neck where he'd fed. Pleasure spiked and she wiggled her ass, clenching her pussy around his cock again.

"Oh, Goddess." Drake groaned, but he didn't sound in pain. "I'm going to slip out here soon and make a mess. Give me a moment and I'll cater to your lovely body."

He rolled them over until he rested his slim hips between her legs and stared down at her breasts. He dipped his head to take one nipple into his mouth and she hissed with pleasure as his tongue helped the peak grow taut.

"I didn't get a chance to taste these this time and I couldn't resist."

He grinned as he pulled his cock from her and stood up. The end dripped with their combined releases as he turned and padded to her bathroom.

"There are some towels in the linen closet just inside the bathroom door."

"Thank you."

She heard the squeaky hinges open and the water run as he found what he needed. He returned to the bed and tenderly cleaned the cum from her nether lips with gentle, but thorough strokes. She gave him a lazy smile, enjoying his nakedness as he strode back to deposit the washcloth in the sink.

"You're very handsome, Drake." She admired his athletic torso and the scars decorating it. "Are the scars from before you became a vampire?"

His steps faltered a little as he came back to the bed, but he helped her under the covers before he slid in beside her. He gathered her against his naked chest and she snuggled closer to his furred heat.

"Yes, my…first life wasn't easy or particularly pleasant, especially toward the end. I was held captive as a child and I fought them any chance I got. These are badges of my struggles."

His voice held wariness and sorrow, and she almost asked more about it, but decided she didn't want to tarnish the lovely feeling of cuddling her True Mate.

"Fortunately, we're here, now, safe and warm in my bed, and the past is where it belongs."

Drake chucked as she nuzzled his chest. "True enough. You're truly magnificent, Aliandra. I'm honored to be here."

"Good. Remember that because I'm expecting you to be here more often."

He chuckled again and reached up to turn off the beside lamp without a word. Aliandra sighed happily and allowed the lovely scent of sex and the sound of his breathing carry her off to sleep.

CHAPTER EIGHT

Drake wandered through his duties the two next days, sated and content. His vampiric hunger didn't hound him at all. *That's because you fed from a dragon, numbskull. Fucked her, too.* He hadn't seen Aliandra since he'd apologized, but they'd both been busy. Her with patients at the clinic, him with the food drive being held at the library for the Little Hands homeless shelter in time for Thanksgiving.

Despite the euphoria, reality slowly seeped into his contentment and guilt led the charge. *Dragon, you fed from and fucked a dragon.* Not the most honorable way to treat the most noble of creatures, and the mascot of his knightly Order. *And she expects me to be there more often.*

"But libraries are booorrrrrinnng, Mom." The whining voice dragged Drake's attention from the pile of books he needed to have Bailey catalog and his guilty thoughts.

That isn't Tom, is it?

A different little boy pouted when his mother tried to coax him to read quietly.

"Boring?" Drake asked as he leaned on the table beside them. The boy glowered. "Libraries are full of strange worlds and adventure. Have you read the *Chronicles of*

Narnia? Slung magic with Harry Potter? Slayed dragons with the Hobbits of the Shire?"

"What's a hobbit?"

"What's a hobbit?" He shot a mock-horrified look at the boy's mother, who smothered a laugh behind her hand. "Dear me, we need to remedy this situation immediately. Step into my office, young man, and I shall tell you all about them."

Drake steered him over to the graphic novel shelves in the children's section. Several of the more famous tales had been made into glorified comic books, told the stories with bright pictures. He pulled out The Lord of the Rings Book One and cracked it open as he sat down beside the boy.

"Now then, a hobbit is a little man, no more than a few inches taller than you, with great hairy feet upon which he never puts shoes."

"Never wears shoes?" The boy shook his head. "He couldn't live with my mom, then. She never lets me go anywhere without shoes."

Drake nodded sagely. "Ah, but he lives in a whole village of people who don't wear shoes, and nothing exciting ever happens to them. Except when a great gray wizard stops by with an adventure full of magic, menace, and Mordor."

He continued to tell the boy all about the Fellowship of the Ring and helped distract himself from his unhappy thoughts. He'd forgotten how much the wonder of children warmed his heart. *Another convert by dinnertime.* He'd like his own child to whom to tell these stories, but he'd have to make do with those who came to the library.

Of course, if he had his choice, he'd like someone like Tom Lance to be his son. There was something special about the boy and Aliandra liked him.

Aliandra. Guilt hit him square between the eyes again and he excused himself from the boy and his mother to return to his office. To his relief, Dr. Lance seemed to have vacated the room for the time being and Drake had the space to himself. He sat down at his desk and took a deep breath.

I should really call Aliandra and thank her for a marvelous evening. But he couldn't make himself pick up the handset on his desk.

Instead, he found the piles of papers and books on the surface distracting and set to organizing them into their proper places. He ignored the voice claiming he only sought to procrastinate from contacting the woman—*dragon*—he'd made love with two days earlier. He didn't entirely regret their intimate moments, but he couldn't help but think he'd overstepped his devotion. *Again.*

Drake had almost convinced himself to pick up the phone when Gemini, their local human-sized fairy without wings, stepped through the Archive doors. She always wore something flowing and diaphanous, even in the winter months. She kept her hair in a traditional pixie cut and her bright turquoise eyes seemed to hold a wisdom her sparkly personality belied.

"Good afternoon, Drake. I have something for you." Gemini grinned widely and held out an iridescent envelope.

"Thank you. What is it?" He took the envelope and little sparks fell off in twinkling cascades, care of her magic.

"It's an invitation." Gemini bounced a little, her excitement infectious. "Open it."

Drake pulled apart the flap and lifted out the creamy invitation decorated with autumn leaves. The metallic gold print reflected in the Archive's lights, highlighting the words "engagement party" and "Gemini Sidhe" and "Bruce Boulderson".

"Are you engaged, Gemini? To the sheriff?"

"Yes!" She twirled in a circle and more of the twinkling sparks filled the room. "And you're invited. We'd love for you to be there tomorrow night." She pointed at the card. "It'll be held at the Ironwood Café from nine to midnight. Even if you have to come late, we'll keep the fire burning for you."

"Thank you, Gemini. That's very kind." He gave her a real smile. "Congratulations and felicitations to you and Bruce. I'd be delighted to be there. Have you invited Dr. Cantora?"

Drake thought he'd kept his voice even and merely inquiring, but Gemini's smile turned knowing and she nodded. "Oh yes. The clinic was one of my first stops today. Aliandra said she'd be there." Gemini winked. "Just in case you wanted to know."

"Ah, yes, of course. Thank you." Drake glanced down at the invitation once again.

"You're welcome." She winked again. "All right, I must be off. I have to invite the rest of the Elder Races. See you tomorrow." The fairy whirled away in a swish of diaphanous skirts and sailed out the door.

Drake leaned back in his chair, tapping the invitation on his thigh. He stared at the phone and wondered if he should call Aliandra. *It has been two days.* Despite his busy schedule, he couldn't stop thinking about her and the amazing thing she did with her teeth and tongue on his cock. *It's only been two days.* He knew she'd been busy and didn't want to intrude. *And more than likely she'll be at the party...if she doesn't avoid it because I'm there.* They hadn't parted on bad terms, but she'd made no more effort to see him than he had to see her. Now he was stuck playing the waiting game and indecision gnawed at him.

To hell with it. Drake rose and threw himself into the archives to organize some documents, ignoring the voice calling him a coward.

****

Aliandra sliced through the air on a rare clear morning

just as the sun crested the edge of the horizon. The light played with the wind and together sang a duet as old as time, soothing some of her sorrow and frustration. She tipped over on one of her wingtips and sailed out over Lake Superior, watching the sunlight glint on the edges of the whitecaps. Clouds threatening a storm hung far to the north. *Looks like the Ice Demons are getting ready for another blow.* She inhaled, sniffing the currents for weather data, but the air around her smelled cold and calm.

Too bad my heart can't be the same.

She shook her horned head, the feathers snapping in the wind of her flight. It had been three days since she'd seen Drake and she ached for him. *Probably because he's my True Mate and we established the connection.* Established, but didn't act on it. She'd told herself it was because they'd both been busy, but in truth she couldn't stand to see the guilt and disgust in Drake's face when she told him they'd been bound by the True Mating customs of her people.

Frustration burned through her gut and erupted in a plume of flame hot enough to flash the moisture in the air to steam. She sailed through and soared up higher into the sky, admiring the golden light gilding the trees on the shore. She hovered there, trying to take pleasure in the cold air and crystal clear morning, but disappointment at her cowardice stole her joy.

She took a breath to roar out her fury, but swallowed when something on the shore caught her eyes. The parking lot at the trailhead to the lake had been empty when she'd started her predawn flight, but now two small human figures stood in the middle of the asphalt expanse and she caught the flashes of something electronic in their hands.

Damn cell phone cameras. Aliandra folded her wings and dropped toward the lake, hoping she'd moved quick enough to make their pictures blurry. Pulling up at the last moment, she leveled out and soared toward the beach. It remained empty in the dawn shadow of the forest, and she landed softly on all four clawed feet.

She summoned the magic holding her human disguise and shifted back into Dr. Aliandra Cantora del Viento, dressed in her thick winter coat and woolen hat. She stuffed her hands into her gloves as she scuffed up the sands where her claws had imbedded. *No need to give the tourists more Facebook fodder.*

Satisfied the tracks had been obliterated, Aliandra turned her feet toward the path back to town and worried over her problem with Drake. She'd have to tell him they were bound now, but she didn't know how without him running from her. *Maybe he'll figure it out on his own.* She couldn't keep the derisive snort from pluming in the frosty air. *Males haven't been taught how to recognize those sorts of things and he's not a dragon.* She sighed and shook her head as she exited the trees into the parking lot.

"Oh my God, did you see that?" An excited woman waved at her from the back of her Subaru tailgate.

"I'm sorry?" Aliandra blinked in surprise.

"Did you see the huge bird-thing in the sky while on the beach?" The woman waved her cell phone vigorously. "I think I got a picture of it."

"Really?" Aliandra's gut cramped. Had the woman captured a clear shot? There hadn't been much to hide her against the sky. "Can I see?"

"Sure." After deftly finding the picture she sought, the woman handed her the phone. "See it?"

Aliandra took the phone and turned her back to the sun to see the screen clearly. A blurry silhouette of some sort of large bird-like creature showed against the pale sky. The shot showed something, but it had the same quality of the famous picture of the Loch Ness Monster and she breathed a sigh of relief.

"Wow. Are you sure it wasn't an albatross or something? Their wings are really huge and they don't look like any other bird out there." She handed the phone back to the tourist.

"No, it wasn't an albatross. It had a really long tail. Didn't I catch it in the picture?"

Aliandra shook her head and shrugged. "No, but maybe you'll see it again if you go down to the beach. It's really calm down there in the mornings, especially at this time of year."

"Are you sure you didn't hear or see anything?" The woman eyed her suspiciously. "It was really big."

Aliandra shrugged again. "Sorry. Good luck."

She turned her feet to head back to town and sighed. Most of the human residents in Three Lakes were cool with the odd and supernatural events that periodically occurred in town. But every now and again tourists with little or no knowledge of the Elder Races saw or stumbled upon something and had to be persuaded they'd seen nothing. The community of Elder Races worked hard to give everyone plausible deniability, but sometimes accidents happened.

Thank the Goddess they didn't get a clear shot. She'd fed that morning on freshly caught deer across the border in Canada, part of the reason she'd been out so early, and she thanked the Fire Spirits she wouldn't have to shift again for a few days while the tourists visited. *No need to give them more monster sightings.*

She hurried her steps through town toward her cottage and tried to turn her mind to more pleasant thoughts. Like the engagement party that afternoon. She was happy for Gemini and Bruce, but her own heart ached. She should be celebrating an engagement, too. *If I can just explain and convince the groom.* Her spirits sank and she let herself into her home with frustrated sigh. She'd have to tell him eventually, but a joyous party wasn't the place. *Maybe after Thanksgiving.* That way she could still enjoy the holiday.

CHAPTER NINE

Drake pushed open the doors of the Ironwood Café
with a sigh of relief. Dr. Lance had been particularly surly
today and even protested leaving the library when Drake
had closed the Archives. Tom had given Drake an
apologetic look, as if a five year old boy could do anything,
but had tugged at Lance's arm, claiming to be really, really
hungry. No parent was immune to the talents of a whiney
child and Lance finally capitulated, but he'd been clearly
irritated.

Drake had just barely refrained from telling the
pompous ass he didn't give a shit. He had said the man
could work in the main part of the library until closing and
Lance had been somewhat mollified. Drake hadn't cared
and left without a backward glance.

Thank the Goddess that's over.

He'd damn near shoved the man out the door and
locked up in time to make it to Gemini's engagement party.
He told himself it was to wish the happy couple the best
and to visit with friends, but honestly, he needed to see
Aliandra. They hadn't spoken more than a passing hello
since the night he'd made love with her and he'd gotten
desperate.

You could've called, idiot. And he should have, but he would've only apologized and Goddess knew he'd done that enough.

"Hi Drake, glad you could make it." Iris waved as she carried some fruity and likely alcoholic drinks over to a table draped with a lacy white tablecloth. "Can I get you something to drink?"

"No, thank you, Iris." He unwrapped himself from his winter attire and inhaled the fragrant scents of Iris's cooking mixed with Elder Races of all species. "On second thought, if you have some of your hot apple cider, I'd take some of that."

"Comin' right up."

Drake nodded and scanned the room. The tables had been pushed back against the walls to provide more space for dancing and mingling. Food covered two large banquet-sized tables near the kitchen and people clustered around them and the prospective bride and groom.

"Drake." Bruce's voice boomed across the room and Drake wove his way through the guests to him. "Good to see you, man. How is the business of history?"

Drake laughed. "Same old stories. How's the business of local crime?"

Bruce smiled and shrugged his massive shoulders. "Quieter this time of year, thank the Goddess. Although I did get a report of a monster sighting over the lake this morning from a tourist. Something about a huge flying snake-like creature. You wouldn't know anything about that, would you?"

Drake raised his eyebrows. "No, not at all. Nothing like that in the town's local histories. Why?"

Bruce's normally stoic expression creased into a smug smirk. "Oh, I just figured you'd be more familiar with flying monsters of various kinds, especially when they resemble dragons or whatnot." He winked. "You sure you know nothing about it?"

"Dragons?" Drake snapped his mouth shut and eyed the grinning dwarf giant. At eight feet tall, Bruce towered over everyone, but he had a solid gentleness that put most at ease. The grin, however, made Drake shiver. "Why would I know anything about dragons?"

"Really? You're gonna go with that response?" Bruce snorted. "Well, maybe you wanna ask Aliandra about it. She's over there talking with William and Snowsong."

Drake followed Bruce's finger and damn near swallowed his tongue when he caught sight of Aliandra. She glowed in the warm lights of the café and his cock hardened in his pants. As the guest of honor Gemini was beautiful, no question, but Aliandra eclipsed everyone around her.

Oh, Goddess, she's wearing that coral-colored dress again.

Drake's mind filled with images from Kate's wedding when Aliandra had stood beside the bride as she said her vows. She'd glowed then, complimenting Kate's beauty, but stealing his attention more than the bride. His cock stiffed more watching Aliandra chat with Snowsong Lutrenin, an Ice Demon who married the local river selkie. Aliandra laughed at something Snow said and Drake shivered with desire. *Damn, it's been only three days and I still need her.*

"So are you gonna say hello?" Bruce thumped him on the shoulder, breaking Drake's trance.

"Uh, yeah." He cleared his throat and managed a smile. "Yes, I think I shall go do that."

"Good. Women like that."

Drake shot him a surprised look, but the sheriff had switched his attention to some of the other guests. Drake took a deep breath and tried to rein in both his hunger and his dick as he approached Aliandra. Snowsong tipped her white-blonde head to look past the dragon woman and gave him a welcoming smile before she took her leave of

Aliandra.

"Good evening, Doc. How are you tonight?"

Aliandra turned and met his gaze, her own full of both sorrow and relief. He couldn't bear to think of her miserable and did the only thing he could think of to comfort her.

"Would you care to dance?"

"Dance?" She blinked at him, her brows coming together in confusion. She shot a look around the café. "But there's no music."

Before he could think of something to say, someone put in a Celtic music album over the PA system and an easy dance tune flowed out of the hidden speakers.

"There is now. Would you dance with me, Aliandra?"

"I'd be delighted." She smiled and took his hand, and fireworks exploded in the café around them.

He stood there, dumbfounded, the sensation of being in the right place at the right time rooting him to the ground. *She's mine. I want no other, ever.* The thought came out of nowhere and yet, he couldn't deny the validity of it.

"Drake? Are we going to dance?"

Wake up and smell the pavement, numbskull.

"Oh, right. Yes, of course." He smiled, his cheeks tight from disuse. How long had it been since he'd just had fun? He offered her his hand and she followed him onto the dance floor.

Drake wrapped his arm around the small of her back and drew her close as the music shifted into a fun and lively piece that mixed jig with slow dance. He inhaled the delicious scents of her as he steered her around the floor. *Sweet Goddess, she smells better than I remember.*

"Are you going to talk to me or just dance there, staring and sniffing?"

Drake grimaced. "I'm sorry, Aliandra. I…I've missed you."

She gave him a doubtful half-smile. "Have you? You

haven't bothered to talk to me in the last three days, so I'm not quite convinced."

"Ah, yes. I'm sorry about that. I knew you were busy, but I got caught up with some pressing matters at the Archives." Mostly one pressing and irritating matter, Dr. Lance.

"Of course." A frown creased her brow below her elegantly styled hair as she sighed.

"I honestly wasn't sure you'd come to the party since you knew I'd be attending."

Aliandra stared at him for a few beats of the music. "Really? You think I'm that petty to curtail the opportunity to wish my friends well just because of you?" She tilted her head. "Why would you ever think that?"

Drake swallowed hard, feeling her anger like a living thing for the first time. "Because I've been a coward and haven't made the effort to see you after our night together."

Aliandra sighed. "Drake, as much as I'd like to blame you this time, the truth is we've both been busy and using it as an excuse."

He almost stopped breathing. "What?"

She nodded. "Yes, I know you've been avoiding me, but I'm just as guilty of staying away. The thing is I don't want to hear you say you're sorry for being with me. What we shared was too important to me to listen to another apology for it." She shook her head and grimaced. "Maybe this wasn't such a good idea."

Aliandra tried to pull out of his arms, but Drake held fast, his fist tightening on the cloth of her dress at her back. *I guess I should be glad she wore nothing with a zipper.* Although the zipper would have given him a better grip.

"Wait. Don't go yet. I promise won't apologize. You told me you're tired of hearing it."

"I'm tired of hearing you apologize then repeating your actions." Aliandra shrugged, her expression resigned.

"I know. I'm trying to do better, but I can't seem to

stay away from you. And I should."

"Why should you, Drake?" Pain leaked out of her voice and eyes, but he couldn't bring himself to explain.

Drake shook his head. "The specifics aren't important. Just suffice it to say I don't want to dishonor you by taking advantage of you."

Aliandra snorted. "How exactly are you taking advantage of me? As I recall, I was in control the other night."

The memory of her riding him to oblivion settled firmly in his mind and his cock hardened between them. Fortunately, he'd chosen briefs that morning and it kept his errant flesh more or less contained, but it didn't stop his heart from speeding up.

"Yes, well, I promise not to do that again." He gritted his teeth against his heart screaming in protest. "I don't understand it. For all my centuries as a vampire, you'd think I'd have learned some form of control over my wayward desires. But I can't stop myself from wanting you, needing you."

Aliandra groaned in frustration. "Has it occurred to you that I might need you as well?"

"*You* need me?" Hope warred with surprise. He wanted it to be true. "What could you possibly need me for?"

Aliandra's expression shifted toward anger and her lips pulled back from her teeth. "So this is all about you and your needs? Did you ever think that maybe I need and want a few things, too?"

"Aliandra—"

"No, stop. I've heard enough." She pulled out of his arms and he tried to hold her, but she used some of her dragon strength to break free. "You know me fairly well, Mr. MacGregor. You know what I feel about our time together. When you can see it's not just about you and your fears then come find me. You keep saying you need to make reparations for actions done long ago. Let me tell you something. *This* is not the way."

Aliandra nodded sharply. "Good night, Mr. MacGregor."

She spun on her heels and strode across the room toward the happy couple celebrating their engagement. Drake watched her go with the ache in his chest growing with each step she took away from him. She never looked back, not once, before she gathered her coat and stepped out of the café into the night.

He might have stood in the center of the floor forever if Kate Blackamber, their resident *Morukai* shaman to the Goddess, hadn't grasped his elbow and steered him to one of the tables. Despite her calming touch, Drake's anguish filled his heart and threatened to spill over.

"Deep breaths, Drake." Kate sat him down at a table and her husband Jayson Wolffe poured him a glass of water. "Drink this and breathe deep." She handed him the water, but Drake could barely choke it down.

By the time he set the glass on the table, he shook as if suffering from palsy. Kate squeezed his hand and dipped her head to catch his gaze. He tried avoiding her, but the lure of her hazel eyes couldn't be ignored.

When he finally met her gaze, she scanned him for a few seconds then nodded. "Oh, so that's how it is."

"That's how what is, Kate?" Jayson sat back in his chair with an amused expression on his face.

"Drake has finally found her." She patted his hand with a wise smile. "Took you long enough."

"What?" Drake blinked.

"Found who?" Jayson asked.

"Found his true mate, his Sacred Love, whatever phrase vampires have to describe their one and only. I can't keep track of all different names the Elder Races have." Kate glanced at her husband. "He's been looking for centuries."

"Aliandra's not my true mate. We're not even the same

species."

Kate dropped her chin and gave him a *you're-kidding-right* look. "You do know Jayson turns fuzzy and needs a chew toy around the full moon, right?"

"Not just around the full moon." Jayson winked and grinned.

"But she's..." Drake shot a look around the café, careful of the humans in attendance, and lowered his voice. "She's a dragon, a sacred creature which my family has revered for generations. It's unethical for me to defile her with my yearnings."

Kate snorted. "Are you listening to yourself? How can you defile someone who likes you? Not only that, she's your true mate, Drake. Your one true love, your princess charming. I know vampires have them because my best friend Bridget is mated to one. He's your nephew as I recall. Fredrick MacGregor?"

Drake nodded. "Yes, I know about Fredrick's marriage to the Avatar of the Goddess."

"Good. So what's the problem here? Aliandra is interested and I'm pretty sure she's in love with you." Drake scoffed and Kate shrugged. "Well, what do I know? It's not like I have a connection to this town or anything."

"I'm sorry, Kate. But in love? With me? It doesn't seem possible."

"Why not? Because you're a broken old vampire who's done so much wrong in his life he can't have anything good?"

Drake stared, sure his mouth hung open like a coffin lid. How did she know exactly what he thought of himself?

"That's the first thing you need to get rid of." Kate patted his arm and gave him a compassionate smile. "You're not broken, I don't think you're that old for vampires, and you've worked hard to replace the bad with a lot of good, Vlad Drakul."

Panic damn near choked him as it swelled in his chest

from the name he'd renounced four centuries earlier. Drake resisted the urge to scream and run for the hills. He scanned the room around them again, sure someone had heard Kate's words and would come for him. But the party continued without pause and laughter filled the brightly lit room.

"How did you know?"

Kate shrugged, completely at ease in the presence of the man known as the fabled Dracula. "I had a cousin who was alive in your time. She lived in the village below your castle and said she always wished she'd done more to help you."

"Help me?" Drake shook his head with a grimace. "I was beyond help."

"Maybe back then, but not now. Not anymore. Rosalisa might not have been able to offer it then, but I can help you now." Kate tipped her chin up and shot him a challenging smile. "You willing to take some friendly and knowledgeable advice from a younger woman despite your advanced age?"

Drake opened his mouth to refuse, but stopped himself. The rule of thumb among the Elder Races stated if the *Morukai* shaman in town had advice, it was best to shut up and listen. "Yes, of course, Kate."

"All right. Here it is. Let go of past actions, because they're in the past. You can't change them and you've more than made up for them." Kate waited for him to nod before continuing. "Look at what you have now, what you've done now, and take what you're being offered. Aliandra can't change the past any more than you can, but she's let it go. She wants you, right here, right now. Your past might be interesting for old stories, but that's all it is. Old stories. It got you to who you are, but it isn't who you are."

Kate grasped his hand and squeezed, meeting his gaze. Drake swallowed hard at the deep intensity in her eyes.

"Do you know why the Elder Races stay in this town?"

He blinked. "They stay because of you, Kate."

"Right. And I stay to help them—to help you—find a clearer path to great things." She shot him a cheeky grin. "The Goddess is all about healing, Drake, and you've done a lot to repair the damage of your former life as Vlad Drakul. But the most important person is still suffering."

He nodded and dropped his gaze. "Aliandra."

"No, you dope. You."

"What?"

Kate sighed and rubbed her forehead. "Why are the Elder Races so damn determined to be miserable?"

Her husband wrapped an arm around her shoulders and chuckled. "Because we get to spend more time with you, then?"

"Shut up." She smacked him on the chest, but her smile returned. "You need to focus on you, Drake, and to have compassion for yourself. Your past actions don't make you unworthy for love. Aliandra is a dragon, but she's also a living being who loves you. Maybe the sacrifice you have to make for her is letting go of all the self-loathing and guilt."

Drake blinked and his gut soured. "How do you know about the sacrifice?"

"Hey, I visit the library, too. I can research. I know about the prophecy and the way to rectify it." Kate sat back, but her expression remained intense. "You need to make a sacrifice to either appease the founder of the Order of the Dragon, or appease a dragon directly. So go do it. Soothe Aliandra's restless heart, sacrifice your addiction to the pain and guilt of your past, and make both of you happy."

Kate didn't wait for him to say anything. Instead, she turned to her husband and patted his shoulder. "I'm ready to go mingle a bit more before heading home."

"All right." Jayson stood up and pulled out his wife's

chair. Kate headed over to the happy couple, but Jayson paused and patted the table. "Take care of yourself, Drake. And I have a suggestion, man-to-man, if you're willing to take one."

Drake eyed the younger man, but nodded slowly.

"Don't fight it. Love isn't nearly as scary as we're led to believe. She's your True Mate, man. Don't make yourself sick avoiding her. It's worth letting go of everything you think is wrong with you just to have her." Jayson shot a loving look toward his wife. "Trust me. She's worth everything. Do yourself a favor and grab onto her with teeth and claws, because being without her fucking sucks." He rapped his knuckles against the table again. "You have a good night. Stop by if you need to talk to either of us."

Drake watched the werewolf saunter over to his wife and wrap his arms around her. Kate smiled and snuggled against Jayson's chest, and Drake's yearning for the same interaction with Aliandra burned in his chest. *But she's a dragon, larger than life, and—*

Kate shot him a look from across the room and shook her head as if she knew the direction of his thoughts. Drake grimaced and stood, desperate to get away from the happiness of the couples around him. He needed to think over what both Kate and Jayson had said because living without Aliandra didn't seem to be an option.

He glanced around for her, but he recalled she'd left him standing on the dance floor. His stomach dropped in disappointment, but he mustered up a smile for Gemini and Bruce as he wandered over to say goodbye.

"You headed out, Drake?" The dwarf giant shook Drake's hand with a meaty paw.

"Yes, it has been a long day and I have to do some research tonight."

The sheriff snorted. "Never understood constant reading, but I sure am glad there are folks like you to keep the records. Without them, I'd've never worked it out with my family. Thanks for that."

"You're welcome, Bruce. I was happy to help." Drake's smile improved. "Congratulations to you and Gemini. I'm happy for you both."

"Thanks." Bruce lowered his brows almost closing his eyes completely. "You thought about talking to the doc about your problem?"

Drake blinked. "Problem?"

"Yeah. The one that's making you glower more than usual and makin' you heartsick. You know what I mean?" Bruce dipped his chin and stared out from under his brows.

Bloody hell, does everyone know about me and Aliandra? He shot a look at Gemini, but the fairy spoke with some other attendees while Bruce focused on him.

"Yeah, most of us Elder folks have noticed, but we didn't want to push or pry. But you're miserable and we know it. See the doc and get fixed up." He shook Drake's hand again. "Thanks a lot for comin' to the party, Drake. It was great to see you."

"Thanks for inviting me and congratulations again. Have a good Thanksgiving, Sheriff."

"You, too."

Drake shrugged into his coat and wrapped his scarf around his neck as he headed toward the door. He nodded to people he passed, but kept his focus on getting out. He really needed time to think and he couldn't do that around so many people. He also needed to feed, but the thought of human or animal blood actually turned his stomach. A bad problem for a vampire.

No, the real problem is I only want Aliandra's blood.

He stepped out onto the cold sidewalk and sniffed the air. The scents of wet concrete, ice, and cold metal met his nose, but the scent he really wanted had fled. The smells of spicy chocolate and burning mesquite wood. Aliandra's scents.

Drake shook his head and trudged to the side door to head home, ignoring the cold wind cutting through his jacket. Could he really love a dragon, and make up for the evil decisions of his past? Kate and Jayson seemed to think so. He shoved open the door and stomped up the stairs. He wanted to scoff, but that took him down old and worn thought lines. The *Morukai* existed to help the Elder Races find the best path, and if she said he needed to let his old fears and faults go, he'd be wise to heed her advice.

When have I been very wise recently?

Another voice piped up, *No time like the present to start.*

He grunted with resignation and grudging agreement. *But first I have to tell Aliandra about who I really am.* And that thought made him throw off his coat and head for bed.

****

Viggo sat back in his chair with a grim smile of satisfaction. All the years of following miniscule leads and strange occurrences had paid off. He'd found the source of the evil, the greatest demon next to an Antisaint. Vlad Tepeş Drakul, the Scourge of Transylvania.

And he's right here in this pathetic little town.

Viggo closed his eyes and let the pleasure mix with relief. It had been decades since he'd started this quest, taking on the sacred name of Vigilance and the hugely important quest to track down one of the most heinous evils the world had suffered.

Literary types named it *Dracula*, but Viggo knew him as the true historical creature. Vlad the Impaler, a man damned to become a soulless nightcrawler for his evil crimes. The stories said the hunters had killed it, but he'd known better. Viggo had even traced the lines of tale about Van Helsing and the Bloody Countess, but they'd led him to dead ends.

He chuckled at the irony. *Dead ends...soon.*

Soon he could take up his mantle of Vigilance again for other pursuits and help his brothers, his fellow Blades of the Sword of God, rout out other evils in the world. *Once I've cleansed this town of the Scourge of Transylvania.* He'd protect these poor people and return to the bosom of the Blades.

A smug smile curled his lips as he logged off the computer terminal and tucked his notes into his courier bag. The library had emptied and only the ditzy clerk remained behind the reference desk. The little brat he'd harbored sat in the Children's Section, but after Viggo had finalized his plans, he'd drop Thomas at the Little Hands Shelter here in Three Lakes. He'd be done with the role of father and researcher. Free to convene with his brother Blades and pursue something new.

Now all I need to do is set a trap. But it would take just as much effort and research as tracking down the Scourge. It was one thing to say he could trap the worst vampire the world had ever known, but quite another to actually do it.

Perhaps he could use the brat to lure him in. The Scourge seemed to like the boy. The vampire hid right under everyone's noses here in the library, claiming to be the archivist and probably feeding on the poor souls who came to get some reading material. Viggo shoved his papers in to his case a little harder than necessary.

Soon. Soon I'll have that soulless bastard staked and beheaded. He shook his head and grabbed small pad of paper to write down his list of materials.

"Garlic, salt, nylon rope, duct tape, zip ties, holy water..." He wrote them in code so no one would understand if they should get his list before he was ready. He had other tools he wouldn't list, but he reminded himself to grab them. *Blessed sword, night-stick, ceremonial cross, holy herbs for the fire.*

Footsteps made him stuff the list into his pocket as he

looked up. The pretty and plump library clerk paused at his table and gave him a vapid smile.

"It's almost time to close up. Are you almost done, Dr. Lance?"

"No, no, that's quite all right. Thomas must get a good night's rest." He rose and threw his coat over his shoulders. "Thank you for your time."

"Are you done with your research?" She gathered up the last of the errant books left out by a previous patron.

"Very nearly. Has Thomas chosen any books to take from the children's section?"

"Not today. Congratulations on being almost done."

"Thank you." He gave her a real smile. "I hope to help the world with it one day."

"That's wonderful. Best of luck with that, Dr. Lance."

It won't take luck, but patience and skill. He nodded, gathered up the brat, and waved goodbye. Soon he'd save this little town from their invisible horror. No one would ever know, but he would and so would the Holy Lord.

CHAPTER TEN

Three flaming days since the party and Drake can't be bothered to say a damn word to me? To be brutally honest, she'd told him to stay away until he'd gotten his shit together. *Apparently that hasn't happened yet.*

Aliandra sighed as she tottered on her boots with three-inch heels. "I so picked the wrong day to wear these."

She wobbled to a stop beside the sheriff, skidding a little in the snow. Bruce grabbed her arm to steady her.

"Thanks. What have we got, Sheriff?"

"Well, near as I can tell, this young fella got a little too deep into the grog and thought the road extended onto the unfinished pier." He shook his shaggy head. "Don't know how he got between the fence and the support beams, but there you go."

"Any injuries other than the driver?"

"Nope. No one else around."

"That's good." She strode for the pier, Bruce following her.

"Hey, I saw you dancin' with Drake MacGregor at the engagement party. He seems kinda sweet on you."

Girlish delight shot through Aliandra, but she only shrugged. "I wouldn't go that far."

"Uh-huh." He leveled a shrewd look at her. "You should give the guy a chance."

She snorted. *I did* give *him a chance. Several.*

"You know, Doc, there are only two tragedies in life: one is not getting what you want, and the other is getting it."

Yeah, but which will I regret more?

She said nothing as they approached the driver who slouched on the icy sidewalk, woozily staring at his truck. Aliandra crouched before him and tried not to gag from the alcohol funk wafting off him.

"Sir, I'm Dr. Cantora. I'm going to check you for injuries."

"Help a brother out. I gotta get my truck."

"Sir, you're going to need to stay still." She caught his shoulder as he listed dangerously sideways. Thank the Goddess she wore leather gloves. She could always burn them later. *Especially with all the alcohol oozing off him.*

Aliandra dug a penlight out of her coat pocket and shined it in the drunken man's eyes.

"Hey, dude, what the fuck?"

"Please hold still." She tightened her grip when he tried to jerk away. She glanced up at Bruce. "No sign of concussion, but he's too out of it to tell right away." She focused on the drunk. "I'm going to check your limbs for damage. Anything hurt?"

"Yeah, man, my ass hurts from sitting on this frickin' sidewalk. I gotta get my truck and drive home."

"You won't be driving anywhere. Not in my town," Bruce rumbled.

"Fuckin' pig! I don't need you to tell me what to do."

Aliandra chuckled. "Wrong species. What's your name, sir?"

"I ain't telling you with the pig around."

Bruce rolled his eyes and held out the man's driver's license. "Anthony Henner."

"Dude, it's Tony the Tiger." Anthony rolled his head toward Aliandra and leered. "Rawr."

Aliandra ignored him as she ran her hands over his lower limbs. Nothing felt broken.

"Hey, you can feel me up a little higher, sweetheart, I don' mind."

She'd been so frustrated with Drake's determined ignorance of her presence for the last few days, she was tempted to thump him in the crotch. She reminded herself she'd taken the Hippocratic Oath and couldn't intentionally do harm.

"He's fine to move. I think you can take him to the cells and have him sober up. We'll deal with him tomorrow when he's coherent."

"Hey, baby, that's all you're gonna do? I was just gettin' warmed up."

She growled low in her throat, but stood up without kicking Anthony in the balls. "He's all yours, Sheriff."

"Come on, Mr. Henner. Let's get you a nice, concrete cell to sober up in." Bruce jerked the man to his feet and dragged him off to a squad car.

Aliandra hobbled toward her own car, slipping and sliding on her heels, grateful she could go somewhere warm. Hopefully, the car hadn't cooled off too much while she dealt with the idiot on the pier.

Her foot hit a patch of black ice and slid out from under her. She gasped and fell, bracing for pain. The scents of rich coffee and pine trees enveloped her at the same moment someone caught her, halting her fall. Heated breath warmed her face and she instinctually grabbed her rescuer.

"I've got you, Aliandra."

Drake's voice seeped into her awareness, bringing comfort and relief, along with need. She wanted to snuggle into his arms and never let go.

If only I didn't have to.

But reality hit her between the eyes and she recalled

his withdrawal the last time they'd been this close. She inhaled slowly to take his delicious scent with her before she pulled back from him.

"Thank you for the save, Mr. MacGregor." She pulled herself out of his embrace and straightened her clothes. "What are you doing out here today?"

"I came to—"

"Apologize, right? Again?" Aliandra shook her head and pushed past Drake to her car. "Better than an apology would be for you to just stay away from me. Then you wouldn't have to keep saying you're sorry you're with me."

She didn't think vampires could go any whiter, but Drake's skin mimicked the snow on the ground around them.

"I'm not sorry when I'm with you, which is the problem."

"That's a problem?" She bit back a snarl. "Oooh, I get it. It's like a hangover. You only regret me in the morning after, right? Just leave me alone, Mr. MacGregor. I don't have the time to waste on players. I'm too damn old."

She dropped into her front seat and slammed the door just as he opened his mouth to respond. *He could be the one who fulfills your dreams of family.* Aliandra snorted and bitch-slapped her bleeding heart. "Not when he regrets every time he touches me. I won't be a guilty pleasure."

She started the ignition and threw the car into gear, but Drake leapt over the hood like an action-adventure star. He jerked her passenger door open so hard the metal protested.

"What in the Goddess's name are you doing?" Fury rumbled in her gut and she held back the urge to torch him in the seat. "Get out of my car."

"No, I'm not going to let you go without understanding why I'm having trouble with you."

"You're having trouble with *me*?" Her canines extended as she peeled her lips back from her teeth. "Get. Out. Of. My. Car."

"No." He bared his own long canines. "You will hear me out, Aliandra Cantora del Viento. If after my explanation you still wish me to go, I will leave you in peace forevermore."

Fury built into a roar that shook her windows and her hands damn near broke the steering wheel off the column. "You have no right to make demands of me!"

"You're right, but I need to explain this to you."

"Why? Why should I listen to you?"

"Because I love you." His expression filled with such haunted distress she recoiled. *Somehow disgusted remorse isn't all that romantic.*

"I'm sorry. Evidently that's a fate worse than death."

He grimaced. "Sorry, that didn't come out the way I meant it. But I need to tell you this, I need to explain." He sighed. "And I've probably made the situation worse in my efforts to avoid the problem."

She stared at him sure he'd lost his mind. "Ya think?"

"Please, Aliandra. Can we go somewhere and talk? There's an important matter I need to speak to you about, and it would be nicer inside."

Aliandra wished she could shift and blast the frustrating vampire into ash, but she didn't want to ruin her car. "No. You can talk here or you can get out. Either way, I don't care."

Drake sighed. "Very well." He bit his lip, one canine compressing the full flesh and teasing her with its beauty. *Focus on him, not his lovely fangs.*

"I'm sure you've heard the stories told of Vlad Tepeş, the Transylvanian Prince who went insane for the love of his wife and eventually evolved into Vlad Drakul, the most hated vampire of all time."

"I know the tale."

"Yes, Bram Stoker had a field day with it. What is lesser known about Vlad is what he did after that horrendous story." Drake turned his gaze out the window to watch the retreating police cars. "He went into hiding and tried to repent for his evil deeds, making reparations everywhere he could. His father was the first to be knighted into the Order of the Dragon and Vlad's heinous crimes had defiled its sanctity. Vlad went into hiding, trying to live small and quiet."

Aliandra started to connect the dots. "How small and quiet?"

"Quiet enough to move to a little town in Michigan to start over."

She took a few breaths to wait for him to laugh. "You're Vlad Drakul? The model for Bram Stoker's Dracula?"

Drake grimaced. "Yes, and I must restore the sanctity of the Order by either making reparations to the order's founder—"

"Who's dead."

Drake nodded. "Or sacrifice myself for a dragon."

Aliandra raised an eyebrow. "What kind of sacrifice?"

"It didn't say." He shook his head. "But that's what's wrong with my love for you. It's beautiful, but it's flawed, and I don't wish to defile you as well."

Her words erupted in a growl. "Did it ever occur to you that your love might *be* your sacrifice?"

He blinked, his expression puzzled. "How could it be? It only brings me pleasure."

"Is that so? You take pleasure in avoiding me, in rebuffing my advances, in running away?"

"No, not at all."

"Then maybe the sacrifice you're looking for is the expectation of what's defined by defilement. Maybe the sacrifice is your fear. Maybe you should stop running away, Drake."

He stared at her for several moments, his eyes wide in the darkness.

"You know, I asked you to bite me, to take

nourishment from me because I knew you needed it, and because I wanted you to have it." She glared her fury at him because the scent of charred flesh never came out of car upholstery. "It brought me pleasure, not only feeling your fangs in me, but being able to give you something you needed. And I know you enjoyed it. I felt it. But now you apologize. Every. Single. Time. Do you understand that hurts more than this imagined slight?"

"Aliandra—"

"No. Don't apologize again. I don't want to hear it. Just get out of my car, think about your choices, and hopefully I'll see you at Thanksgiving supper on Thursday."

"You still want me to come to Thanksgiving?" Drake blinked like a big white owl.

"Yes, if you get your priorities straight. You don't want to dishonor me? Fine, don't eat and run. Now get out."

Drake wore an expression of bewildered hurt, but Aliandra refused to care. *Take your medicine, vampire. Doctor's orders.* He slid out of her car and shut the door, staring at her through the window. She threw the vehicle in gear and pulled away from the curb, gritting her teeth against the fire brewing in her belly. She'd have to take a flight and let off some of her rage or she was liable to burn down the clinic while on call.

That wouldn't go over well with the locals.

****

Drake stood on the curb in the gently falling snow and watched Aliandra drive away. *Your love might be your sacrifice.* Kate had said the same thing. Well, not about the love, but about the fear and guilt over loving Aliandra.

Yet she still wants me to come to Thanksgiving dinner. The amazement damn near staggered him and he shuffled back toward the library from the pier. Could he do it? Could he let go of Vlad Tepeş for good and leave the hurt, frightened, and angry young man he'd been in the past where he belonged?

Snow peppered the sidewalk and his chest as he walked into the wind. The scent of cold, wet concrete filled his nose, but his churning thoughts warmed him as he trudged along. The wind whistled through the buildings as he shoved his frigid hands into his pockets.

In truth, he'd been Drake MacGregor longer than he'd been Vlad Tepeş Drakul, and he'd spent far longer doing reparative work in compensation. Hell, he'd even taken in a few new vampires and taught them how to survive without killing. And now he had the opportunity to continue his penance by loving an actual dragon, a woman who lit his fire and warmed his heart more than his wife Ilona had at their wedding.

Much more so. His strides lengthened as the fire bloomed in his chest and purpose spread to his limbs. It was time to let all of the past go and take something good for himself and for his Order. The Order of the Dragon had been founded to stave off the Turks back in the day, but now it stood for honoring the good in the world. He'd need to write an archival note, an entry to explain how the prophecy had been served. And then he needed to find Aliandra and make good on his statement of love.

By the time he reached the library's doors, he felt better than he had in centuries. The guilt and sorrow had sloughed off and he found a new purpose in his life. He hadn't figured out all the ways he would put it into practice, but past actions could no longer dictate the present. A smile cracked his lips as he threw himself into the warmth of the library's silence.

Some of his motivation faded as a rank scent hit his nose. *Dear Goddess, has someone left a rotting thing in the trash somewhere?* He paused and scanned the stacks. No one had stayed this late except Dr. Lance and Tom, but maybe the janitorial staff had missed something noxious. Drake ducked behind the circulation desk to check the trash cans, but only fresh bags greeted him.

He frowned and systematically walked the stacks, sniffing for the source of the odor. He found Tom in the kids' section, but only waved as he tracked the stench. It seemed to be intensifying toward the Archival office. *You have to be kidding me. Did Lance leave something to rot in my office?* Drake strode for the Archives doors, wondering why the man had shut them.

He grasped the handles on the doors and pulled them open. A blast of brilliant light and stench streamed over him. Drake threw up his arms to cover his eyes as he nearly gagged on the air reeking of garlic and rotten meat. A hideous droning accosted his ears as he recoiled, but before he could get out of the blazing smell, something crashed into the back of his skull.

Drake dropped to the floor with a shout, seeing stars and swallowing bile. *What the fuck?*

Before he could scramble up, someone tackled him back down and wrenched his arms behind him. A voice muttered something so full of evil, Drake gagged again.

"Be still, foul beast. Thou art mastered." The thick, rancid voice coated his skin and the man slammed him to the floor as he bound Drake's hands behind him in wet, hard nylon rope. "For thou shalt be cleansed from this town and this world, and thy soulless muck shall be cast out. Though I cleanse the world of thee, I'll play the harlot no longer than necessary. Thy filth shall be purged and humanity will be saved."

"What the fuck are you talking about?" Drake struggled, his fangs cutting through his gums as his fury rose. "Get off me!"

"Silence!"

The blow to the back of his head ensured it.

CHAPTER ELEVEN

"Aliandra!"

The high scream preceded a small body hurtling through the clinic's doors and straight into her arms. The rancid scents of fear, anger, and frustration tinged with garlic hit her nose.

"Tom? What's wrong?" She caught the dragonet and held him while he shuddered against her belly.

"He took him!" Tears stained Tom's face as he looked up at her, his silver-gray eyes panicked.

"Who took whom?"

"Viggo! Viggo hurt Mr. MacGregor and took him out of the library. You have to help him."

"Calm down and start at the beginning. Here, sit down for a moment." She pulled him over to one of the rolling stools. "Now tell me everything that happened?"

"I was in the library when Mr. MacGregor came in." Tom gulped air as more tears streamed down his face. "He didn't look very happy, but he waved to me as he went by. I got up to see what was wrong when I heard him shout and a loud noise." Tom shook his head. "I crept closer because it sounded like Viggo was chanting something bad at Mr. MacGregor. The words made my ears hurt." He rubbed his ears like they still ached.

"Go on. What happened next?" Aliandra could guess, but she wanted to hear it as the fury inside shifted from Drake to Dr. Lance.

"Viggo dragged Mr. MacGregor out of his office by his arms. Mr. MacGregor was bleeding really bad from his head. I hid behind the library counter because I didn't want Viggo to see me. He looked bad, Aliandra."

"Bad? Like he was sick?"

Tom shook his head. "No, like mean-bad, like he was gonna do something horrible to Mr. MacGregor." He tugged on her coat sleeve. "You have to help him, Aliandra. Please. He's in trouble."

"I will. I promise, Tom, but I need you to do something for me."

Tom sniffled. "What?"

"I need you to run as fast as you can to Iris Maple at the Ironwood Café and tell her what you told me." Aliandra stood up and pulled off her doctor's coat. "I need you to tell her Viggo took Drake somewhere and I'm on my way to help him. Can you do that?"

"I-I-Iris?"

"Yes. She's the Queen of the Dryad's Garden and she'll be able to find Drake quicker than I can. Can you do that for me, Tom?"

He nodded vigorously. "What are you gonna do, Aliandra?"

"I'm going to go out there and bring him back safe. Don't worry." She threw off her three-inch heels and strode for the front of the clinic. Tom trotted after her, his bottom lip between his teeth. *Let's hope no one needs the doctor while I'm out.* Who was she kidding? Drake needed the doctor more than anyone at the moment.

Aliandra paused at the doors, taking in the damp night. The snow had started after she returned to the clinic and now a light mantle of white decorated the steps and railings. The snow would make it easier to follow on the ground, but harder to locate the men from the air. *Fortunately, I know my Mate very, very well.*

She crouched in front of Tom and zipped up his coat. "Do you remember where the café is?"

"Yes. Just two streets down from the library."

"That's right. You run there as fast as you can and bang on the door, even if it's locked. They'll hear you and come to see what's wrong." She cupped his cheek. "You get to be the hero you couldn't be for your family, Tom. You'll save everyone tonight."

"I don't want to be a hero, I just want Mr. MacGregor back."

"We have to work together to make that happen. Now go, quick!"

The little boy ran off into the snow, his small footprints trailing behind him in black relief. Aliandra made her own tracks into the snowy dark, striding for the open parking lot of the clinic. No cars filled the fading stalls and she'd have all the room she'd need to shift into her natural form.

I'm coming for you, Drake. Have faith in me. She took a few running steps and let her true form burst out of her human disguise. Great wings if iridescent green slapped the air as her scaly hindquarters shoved off from the icy ground. Intense joy always followed her transformation into the body she knew best, but tonight, it hardened into billowing fury. Her Mate had been captured and Goddess knew what the evil man had planned. But she'd be damned before she let anything happen to Drake.

She'd fall out of the sky like a blazing star, her fiery breath clearing the way. *No one hurts my Mate but me. That demon-excrement will die.* She'd make sure of it.

****

Drake swam back to consciousness and swallowed

hard against nausea. His head rang with throbbing pain and he dragged a hand up to his head. Except it wouldn't move. Nor would his other arm. Opening his eyes took all his energy and willpower. Nothing would focus for a few moments, but the ropes binding his arms and ankles became solid enough.

Not ropes. Cables.

Steel cut into the skin at his wrists and ankles, cold with the decreasing temperatures of the wintery night. He tested the bonds, but he had no leverage to use his superior strength. Whoever had tied him knew how to disable one of the Elder Races efficiently.

Whoever had tied him... Drake frowned and scanned the space around him. The only light came from a Coleman lantern set on top of a snow-flecked boulder, and cast flashing shadows as more snow fell through its glow. He stood tied to a bare snag in the center of a recent clearing of the forest.

Oh, the dryads won't be pleased about that.

Iris came across as a sweet, mellow lady until someone harmed her trees. Drake shrugged his shoulders to ease the ache, but the cables at his wrists had been secured to something anchored in the snag and he couldn't move them at all.

He frowned deeper and searched his memories of the evening's activities. He'd spoken with Aliandra in her car until she kicked him out because of his determined misery. Drake grimaced and shook his head, but the motion made him gag and he stopped. *Focus on the memories...*

Kate Blackamber had given him the key to fixing the rift between him and his dragon lady, and after he'd talked to Aliandra, he'd gone back to the library to write down his decision and how it pertained to the prophecy. *What happened then?*

Black energy had swirled out of his office, combined with a chant of horrific intent. He'd only stepped through the door when the energy made him sick to his stomach and someone hit him over the head. The evil sounding chant followed him down into the blackness.

Who the hell would be in the library at that hour?

The memory of Tom surfaced and Drake's gut sank. *Dr. Lance.* That's who waited in his office for him. That's who'd hit him over the head. *Who the hell is this guy?*

Motion out of the corner of his eye made Drake roll his head to the left. The subject of his thoughts crouched beside the boulder where he'd dug a pit and surrounded by rocks. He struck a lucifer and lit the kindling doused with lighter fluid in the pit. *They call them matches now.*

Flames lit the clearing, hissing and snapping as the flakes of snow drifted into its flickering tongues. The light painted Dr. Lance's face in ghastly shadows, but the burning glare in his eyes came from within. *Holy Goddess, he looks like a fanatical priest.*

Lance wore long black robes with purple vestments embroidered with ancient religious symbols. He couldn't see clearly in the flickering light, but he thought he saw a cross and a chalice as the man turned toward him. Lance had grown pale and gaunt over the days he'd visited and Drake's skin crawled when the other man came close.

"It has taken many, many centuries to catch up with you, evil one." Lance swung an incense burner past the snag where Drake stood. "And many decades of my own time to find where you'd made your new lair. But my research and patience has paid off, and I now have you where you can be destroyed once and for all."

"What in blue blazes are you talking about? I'm the town archivist and historian, Dr. Lance." Drake pitched his voice so it would carry over the roaring flames, but the weakness in it wasn't completely feigned. His head pounded and his stomach threatened to heave the dinner he'd eaten before meeting Aliandra.

"Enough of your lies, foul one!" Lance swept the

incense burner closer and Drake coughed with the sickeningly sweet stench. "I know who you truly are. I've seen your works of terror and abomination throughout history. I've followed them down through the ages until I tracked you here to this quaint little town. You've hidden yourself very well, Vlad Tepeş Drakul, but I know who you are and what you've done."

Drake's gut clenched and his nausea surged, but he tried to keep his expression bewildered. "I told you, I'm the arch—"

"Enough!" Lance swung the incense burner at Drake. He tried to duck, but the cables held him fast and the censor slammed into the side of his head. "You can't fool me anymore, foul creature. You will pay for your sins and the innocent lives you've taken. As a member of the elite Blades of the Sword of God, I shall smite thee and send thee to hell."

Sweet Goddess protect me.

He'd heard of the Sword of God. It was a fanatical religious group bent on eradicating all the Elder Races from the world. And they'd come to Three Lakes before in an attempt to kill Kate Blackamber, claiming she was some sort of demon.

And now they're here for me.

Drake swallowed hard as Lance drew a sword covered in symbols similar to those on his vestments. He raised it over his head and chanted in some hideous sounding language, words that hurt Drake's ears and turned his stomach. Lance waved the sword a few times before holding it over the open flames and heating up the blade.

"Now, foul beast, thou shalt feel the pain of the innocent and burn for thy heinous crimes." Lance swung the blade toward Drake. "I name thee once only, Vladimir Drakul, the Scourge of Transylvania, the Defiler of the world, the worst of all the demonkin, and I shall cleanse the world of thee tonight."

Without another word, Lance thrust the sword straight into Drake's gut. Searing heat exploded through his awareness followed by excruciating pain. Drake screamed his fury and agony to the night air full of powdery flakes. He writhed against the cables holding him, but the pain wouldn't end and he couldn't get away.

"Burn, thou wicked thing. May God have mercy on those you've destroyed." Lance's eyes glowed with feral delight as he twisted the sword into the wooden snag behind Drake, tearing through muscle and bone.

Drake closed his eyes as he ran out of breath to scream. He wouldn't give this bastard the satisfaction of hearing his agony. Instead, he tried to pull his awareness away from the livid pain in his gut. *The body is not me. I'm beyond the pain. I'm stronger.*

The words were as old as the ruins of his father's castle, but tonight they couldn't hold his attention any more than they had as a child. Tonight Drake reached for any comfort, any hope, any connection to bring him solace as a madman rained hatred and insanity on him.

Sweet Goddess, help me. Forgive me for my mistakes and give my love to Aliandra. He'd meant to see her after he annotated the histories, to tell her he loved her and would never run from her again. *But now she'll never know I've changed my mind.*

Regret deeper than he'd ever felt tore through him and tears leaked out of his eyes. Not for the pain inflicted by the crazy human, but for the hurt he'd caused Aliandra. *I should've just let it all go and stayed with her.* Lance's expression turned triumphant at the tears, but Drake ignored him. He couldn't hurt Drake more than he'd hurt himself. *I was a fool.*

"Do you repent, foul beast? Do you beg God Himself for your salvation?" Lance spat the words, flecks of spittle spotting his lips as we waved another blade through the flames. "It's too late. There is no salvation for the likes of you."

Drake panted, the sword through his gut screaming pain through him as it pinned him to the big snag. He strained against the bindings holding his hands. His considerable strength faded and he had no leverage to break them.

Aliandra is going to be furious. Drake swallowed a moan. *I'm sorry, sweetheart.*

Lance fixed him with a sharp look, a feral light burning in his eyes. "You're the progenitor, the first, and I've been charged with your demise."

Drake wanted to laugh, but the sword prohibited it. "The first? Not hardly."

Lance sneered. "You can't hide anymore, beast. You're the one they called Dracula all those years ago."

Drake braced himself for the old rush of guilt, but it never came. He'd made peace with his past and had long ago paid for his mistakes. He shot the fool a flat look. "You got all this from Bram Stoker's novel? You know that's fiction, right?"

"I did research. I know the true you. Vampire. The worse evil to ever come upon this earth. And I shall smite thee!" He raised an ornate curved knife encrusted with glittering jewels above his head, the blade glowing dull red from the heat.

Great Goddess, tell Aliandra I love her. He waited for the sear of heat in his throat.

The snap of wings broke through the flames' crackling and they both looked up. The snow had stopped and no stars broke through the flat black sky. But a furious roar shook the clearing and the trees around them as an iridescent green dragon arrowed straight for them.

The great beast back-winged and blew a swath of fire around Lance and Drake, creating a barrier. There'd be no escaping now as the dragon's talons sank into the snow-covered turf. The great wings fanned out the little campfire and only the light of the flame hedge offered any visibility.

Lance gasped and backpedaled as far as he could go without the flames licking at his robes. He clutched the jeweled knife in front of him and gaped as the great feathered head with peacock-green eyes fixed on him. "Dear God, there's a dragon!"

Drake would've laughed at the expression of panic on Lance's face, but he barely had energy enough to keep his eyes open as his life bled away. *She's beautiful in her natural form.* He'd never seen Aliandra as a dragon, but the long, sinuous body with short legs and sharp talons glittering in iridescent glory took his breath away. *Or maybe that's the sword in my gut.*

"Keep away, foul beast!" Lance shrieked, waving the jeweled knife at Aliandra's head.

She hissed, distracting him from her tail snaking around behind him. She swung her head from side to side in a hypnotic rhythm and Lance watched her, unaware of her tail until it slammed into the back of his knees.

Lance pitched forward and Aliandra struck, snapping her jaws over his body. His scream lasted only a few seconds as her teeth met in the middle, cutting him in half. She shook her head, his body flopping like a rag doll until she spat him into the flames and the carcass caught fire. Drake swallowed hard and thanked the Goddess he wasn't the target of her fury. *I wouldn't last much longer than Lance.*

"Aliandra." Drake's voice came out no louder than a whisper, but she turned her glorious feathered head and fixed him with one glittering eye. "I love you. Want you to know before I die."

Normally, swords didn't do much but cause him pain, but this one seemed to curtail his healing process and drain away his energy. The flames around them afforded him some comfort against the winter cold, but he struggled to keep his eyes open as the frigid air stole his heat.

She tipped her head and growled, before closing her eyes. The world seemed to go transparent for a moment and the image of the dragon wavered until it disappeared as if it had never been. Instead, Aliandra the woman stood before him, her expression angry.

"Hold on for me a little bit longer, Drake." She reached for the sword stuck through his gut. "This might hurt, but the sword is draining your life and that just won't do." She grasped the hilt with one hand and placed the other on his shoulder. She hissed in pain, but met his gaze. "Ready?"

He could barely nod.

Aliandra roared as she yanked the sword out of the snag, the flesh on her hand smoking from the corrosive power within the item. She flung the offensive weapon away into the ring of fire around them. The thing shrieked in protest as it hit the flames and flared an evil green before going up in smoke. The stench emitted from the fire consuming the blade made Drake's eyes water as he slumped against the snag.

"How are you doing, Drake? Is that better?"

He rolled his head from side to side. "Too weak. Not healing. So sorry."

"Enough of the apologies. Let me untie your hands and we'll work on the rest. Give me a moment, but stay with me. Drake? Stay with me." She grasped his chin and forced his head up until he met her gaze. "Hold on just a little longer."

He tried to nod, but he couldn't hold his head up without her help.

"I'm going to untie your feet first, then your hands." She darted behind the snag and the bonds around his ankles loosened and fell away. "Just your hands left and you'll be free." She snapped the cables around his wrists as if they'd been made of string and he crumpled to the ground with a hollow grunt.

"Oh, Drake." Aliandra gathered him against her chest, hooking her arms under his to pull him close to her throat. "You're going to have to help me, *sa kierna*. Help me help you. You must feed from me if you're going to survive. Come on. I know just a little of my blood does you a world of good."

"So tired…"

"I know you are, but you can't sleep now. You must feed." She shook him a little, but his awareness already slid toward the oncoming blackness. "Please. Please, Drake, feed from me. You must. I need you. I love you, *sa kierna*. Please."

He tried to open his mouth, to sink his fangs into her soft, spicy-scented skin, but the darkness closed in and he lost himself to it.

CHAPTER TWELVE

"Drake?" Aliandra froze as he slid down her body, completely boneless. "Drake." She shook him a little. "Drake!"

Aw fuck. She rolled him onto the ground and scanned his body. The oozing wound in his cut refused to heal and she knew she had to get blood into him. *How in the Hellwinds am I going to do that when he's out cold?*

Blood stained his clothes from his torso down and reeked of rot and death. The ragged edges of the wound showed where the bastard had twisted the blade while it was stuck through Drake's body and fury bloomed in Aliandra's chest.

"You're not getting out of this life so easily, Drake MacGregor." She took a deep breath and sank her canines into one of her arms, slashing open her skin until blood poured from her wound.

She stuck a finger between Drake's teeth and pulled open his jaw as she rested her wound over his mouth and let her blood dribble into it. "You will swallow this gift, Drake. Do you hear me? You owe me so much more than this, but it's a start. You better swallow this."

The blood filled his mouth, but he didn't swallow and

she had to pull her arm back before it overflowed onto the ground. She licked her wound closed and waited, watching him closely to see if he ingested any of the liquid.

"Come on, Drake. Swallow."

She resisted the urge to shake him when the time stretched and the fires began to gutter out. Snow fell from the laden clouds in delicate flakes to decorate his still face and Aliandra's heart began to sink. *Oh please, Goddess, tell me I'm not too late. Please help me save my True Mate.*

"Please, Drake. Drink for me." She dropped her head onto his chest and listened for a heartbeat, but she couldn't hear anything over her own thundering pulse. "Please."

Nothing happened and Drake's body grew colder as the seconds ticked away. Tears leaked from her eyes and she buried her nose against his chest. Fear and despair threatened to swallow her whole and she sobbed against the hard muscles of Drake's torso. *He's too beautiful to leave now.*

She let her tears soak his shirt, but after a few moments she realized her cheek was warm where it met his chest. Aliandra jerked her head up and stared at her mate, trying to discern any movement. Her night vision improved as the fires died and his skin appeared less pale in the darkness. When his throat moved as he swallowed, she whimpered with hope.

"Drake?"

He didn't say anything, but he swallowed again and sucked in a new breath.

"Oh, Goddess. Drake, can you hear me?"

He opened his eyes and searched for her. Aliandra leaned over him and gave him a hopeful smile. "I'm here, *sa kierna.* Do you need more blood? Can you sit up?"

His mouth worked, but no sound emerged, even to her sensitive ears. When she leaned closer, he threw his arms around her shoulders and sank his fangs into her throat. She gasped and jerked, but forced herself to hold still as he fed with deep swallows.

The blood must have worked to not only heal his body but to bring his awareness out of the primal need for food. Drake pulled back just enough to rest his lips against her neck after licking the wound closed. He stayed there, still holding her shoulders in a tight grip, breathing without saying a word.

"Drake?"

"Thank you." His voice sounded like two rusty tin cans rubbing together, but it came out coherent.

Aliandra pushed him back enough to look at the hole in his gut. The blood staining his clothing had stiffened into black tar, but the skin beneath had closed and showed a healing pink scar. Relief flooded through her and she took a deep breath.

"You're welcome. Do you feel well enough to travel?"

"Travel?" He frowned, his gaze sliding around the empty clearing surrounded by glowing embers.

"Yes. I'm going to take you home where you can rest after this ordeal."

He snorted softly, some of his original humor returning. "Not to the clinic?"

She shot him a dry look, happier than ever he was making snarky remarks. "A hungry, injured vampire at the clinic around people with other injuries? Are you insane?"

"Maybe. I'm in love with a dragon after all."

"Yeah, I'd question your sanity there, too." She gave him a smile to take the sting out of her words. "I hope you don't mind flying because that's the fastest way home."

He grasped her arm before she could turn away and met her gaze solemnly. "I love you, Aliandra, beyond time and logic. I'm sorry for the hurt I've caused through my stupidity. I'm done running and I only want to be with you."

Pleasure and relief threatened to spill out her eyes, but she swallowed them and managed a watery smile. "It's about time you figured that out. Now just hold that thought until I get you home and we can talk about it more."

She backed away from him to give her the space to shift into her true form, but before she summoned the energy, a tall, slender woman stepped from between the trees and bowed.

"Gentle rains and breezes to you, Wind Mistress. Queen Iris sends her regards and asks if there is aught else you need."

Aliandra smiled at the dryad messenger. "No, thank you. Thank her for your excellent directions and your timely arrival in keeping the evil contained."

"I will convey your gratitude and tell Her Majesty all is well." The dryad nodded with her own smile before fading back into the trees.

"What did you mean about the directions and containment?" Drake sat up and braced his weight on his arms.

Aliandra tipped her head toward the woods. "The dryads moved the trees in the direction of this clearing like a big terrestrial arrow and if Dr. Lance had tried to make a run for it, he would've found the way blocked by an impenetrable wall of branches and brambles."

Drake blinked. "How did they know where to look?"

"Tom came to the clinic as soon as Lance took you from the library. I sent him to Iris just before I took off." She smiled. "Now, let me change so we can get out of the cold. I'd rather be inside snuggling than out here in this wet storm."

He chuckled and she gathered the energy to shift into her true form. As her body shifted and grew, she reveled in the knowledge of Drake's acceptance. He wouldn't be running from her anymore. *Let's hope that's true when he finds out he's bound to me for the rest of his life.*

She scooped him up in her talons and grinned at him, which made him swallow hard, but he gamely held on as she launched herself into the wintery sky. While she would've loved to show him all the ways she could dance in the wind, she decided summer would be a better season to introduce him to the joys of flying. She focused on getting back to her cottage as fast as possible.

Aliandra set him down at the steps to her back deck before she landed and shifted back into her human shape. She shivered against the cold and hurried up to the porch to find the extra hidden key. "Hellwinds, it's cold out here. Come on, let's get you inside."

She unlocked the door and turned to help Drake inside, but he walked in on his own, and she admired his body through his torn clothes. *There is something seriously wrong with me if I'm thinking how handsome he is while he needs to recover.* She closed the door and hurried to the fireplace to start a fire. She threw the wood into the black sooty maw and blew a little wisp of flame onto the kindling. When the wood caught, she smiled. *Something to be said for being a dragon.*

"Let me get you settled before I go back out." She strode into the kitchen to set the kettle on to boil. "I'll make you some tea first. You should take a shower, too. Warm yourself up."

"You have to go back out?" He raised his eyebrows as he sat down gingerly in one of her fluffy chairs.

"I have to let Tom know you're all right and Lance is gone."

Drake sighed and shook his head. "Lance was Sword of God."

Aliandra stiffened. "Another one? Holy Goddess, and he had Tom all this time. Hellwinds." She shook her head, her anger surging. "Why was he here?"

"He came for me." Drake's shoulders slumped. "He came for Dracula."

She frowned. "What for? You haven't been Dracula for centuries. Why did he come now?"

"He's a terrible researcher?" Drake snorted, but his humor died. "Apparently the Sword of God has me down in the books as the Scourge of Transylvania and the progenitor of all vampires, therefore public enemy number one." He sighed. "Of course, all Elder Races are on their most wanted list, but Dracula was the Holy Grail of their quest to "save" humankind from us."

"That's ridiculous. Most of the Elder Races help humans, or at least live with them peaceably."

Drake nodded. "I know that, and most of this town knows that. Hell, most of the world doesn't know we're even here, but the Sword of God is actively seeking out Elder Races and trying to destroy us."

"Why?" Aliandra gaped at him.

"Who really knows? They're fanatical about it, though."

She shook her head. "That's stupid." Tom's face filled her thoughts and she gasped. "Oh, Goddess, Tom's parents."

Drake frowned. "What about them?"

"Tom said his parents were killed by men claiming to be warriors of God. They must have been Sword of God." She narrowed her eyes and wished she could kill Dr. Lance all over again. *I should've made him suffer more.* But that went against everything she believed as well as her Hippocratic Oath. "And then one of them took him in and brought him here." She growled. "I have to go get him. He has no one."

Drake stood up and wrapped her in his arms. He smelled like blood and winter forest, but his body radiated heat similar to what burned in her gut. "I love you, Aliandra, and I love Tom. Go get him and bring him here. We'll do our best to take care of him and give him a home."

Some of her tension left her shoulders. "You do know he's a dragonet, right?"

"He's a what?"

Aliandra pushed back to look up at him. "Tom's a dragon."

Drake blinked before anger suffused his features. "That sick son of a prick. Lance was one of the ones who killed Tom's parents, wasn't he?"

"I don't know. Probably. How else would he have come across orphaned Tom?" She rested her head against Drake's chest. "I have to give him a home, Drake. He needs to have a family who loves him and understands him. He needs a dragon."

Drake tipped his head to meet her gaze. "And you need a family, a child."

Aliandra blinked, swallowing hard. "How do you know that?"

He sighed. "I'll never be able to give you children, but I've seen how you interact with Tom and other human children here in town. And I'm too old and too selfish to give you up or share you with someone who could give you dragonets." He tucked her hair behind her ears where it had come loose from her braid. "Tom needs you and you need him. Go get your new son and bring him home."

"But what about you? Will you be all right?" She ran her hands over his belly where a pale scar still resided. "Have you healed enough? Do you need more blood?"

"I'll be fine. I'm going to take a shower and make some tea for you." He kissed her forehead and she had the odd sensation of being the smaller being in the room. "If you show me where the linens are, I'll even make up a bed for Tom when he gets here."

She squeezed Drake tight and he chuckled as he squeezed her back. "I love you, Drake."

"I love you, too. Go get Tom and I'll see you when you get back."

She showed him where the linens were for her guest bedroom and stuffed her feet into her snow boots before shrugging into her warm jacket. Drake gave her a hot, sensual kiss before she stepped out into the cold again, and she grinned as the door closed behind her. She had her mate, now she needed to collect her son.

****

Aliandra pulled open the door of the Ironwood Café and looked around for Tom. Iris saw her and waved from a booth closest to the kitchen.

"Where is he?" Aliandra hurried to the table, but only found the boy's jacket.

"He's washing his hands so he can have some pumpkin pie. He's all right. How are you?" Iris looked her over with a critical eye. "I received your message, but I wanted to be sure."

Aliandra sighed and dropped into the booth's bench seat. The old leather creaked in protest as she slid closer to the wall.

"We're okay, but it was a close call. That bastard drove a sword through Drake's gut, and Drake almost died from blood loss." She had to swallow a snarl. "He almost killed my mate, Iris, and he used an ensorcelled sword. It was draining Drake's soul."

"Blight and drought." Fury laced the dryad Queen's voice. "Who was he?"

"Sword of God."

"Sweet Goddess." Iris shook her head. "Why was he here? Why do they keep coming here?"

"He came for Drake, for something he'd done in his past." When Iris raised her rusty eyebrows, Aliandra shook her head. "It's not my story to tell, but that's why Dr. Lance came. The worst part is…" She lowered her voice after scanning the café for Tom. "I think he killed Tom's family before bringing him here."

Iris hissed and the building groaned with her rising

anger. "Is the rotgut bastard dead?"

Aliandra nodded. "Yes. I bit him in half and tossed him in the flames."

Iris smiled. "That should do it." But her face sobered. "What about Tom? What will happen to him?"

Before Aliandra could answer, the patter of small feet sounded on the linoleum and Tom hurried through the tables. "Aliandra? What are you doing here? Is Drake okay? Did Viggo hurt him bad?"

She smiled and grasped his hands, squeezing gently. "You were a hero, my little man. You saved Drake from a terrible fate. I was able to get to him in time. Drake's just fine and he's at my house resting. You did such a great thing tonight, Tom."

She pulled him into a hug and fought back tears. Tears of joy for Drake's survival, tears of sorrow for Tom's loss. *Oh, Goddess, I want this little dragonet for my own. Please let him want to be with me and Drake.* She squeezed him gently then sat back.

"But that means things have changed a little."

Tom's eyes widened and he nodded, swallowing hard. "I understand."

"I don't think you do, so let me explain." She took a deep breath and met his clear silver gaze. "Because Viggo tried to hurt Drake, I had to kill him to stop him. Viggo had gone insane and wouldn't have stopped with just hurting Drake. He would've hurt a lot of the people living in our town and I couldn't let that happen." She bit her bottom lip. "Viggo's dead and gone now."

Tom nodded, but he didn't appear sad. "Okay."

"You're not upset?"

He shook his head. "Viggo wasn't a nice man. I didn't like him."

Aliandra snorted. "No, he wasn't a nice man, but killing him wasn't nice, either. Unfortunately, there wasn't much of an alternative, but now you don't have anyone to look after you."

Tom nodded. "I know."

Sorrow tightened her throat at his resignation, and she had to clear it before she could speak. "So here's my thought on that. How about you come to live with me and Drake, and be our little boy? I could teach you all about being a doctor and flying, and Drake could teach you about history and all the Elder Races. What do you think?"

Tom looked at her a long time and Aliandra started to worry he might turn her down. *Oh, please, let him agree.*

"Are you going to marry Drake?"

Aliandra blinked as Iris gasped in happy surprise. She shot Iris a look before returning her gaze to Tom. "Probably, but not before Yule."

"Will I be able to call you Mama and called Drake Papa Drake?"

She fought a smile as she considered. "You'd have to ask Drake, but I'm okay with you calling me mama."

A wide smile curled Tom's lips. "Okay." He threw himself into Aliandra's arms and hugged her tight. "I'm so glad you're gonna be my mama."

Aliandra choked out a laugh and held Tom tight as tears cascaded down her cheeks. She'd gotten her wish. A family, with Drake as her mate and Tom as her son. *Thank you, sweet Goddess.* She held Tom until he squirmed a little and laughed again as Iris handed her a napkin to wipe her eyes. The dryad Queen winked and offered her a big smile.

"All right. Let's get your coat on and we'll go home. Drake's putting together a nice warm bed for you tonight."

"At your house?" Tom slid his arms into his jacket and pulled his hat on his head.

"At *our* house."

"Yeah, our house." A brilliant smile lit up his a face.

Aliandra wanted to hug him all over again, but she grinned at Iris and ushered the dragonet out the door so they could walk home.

CHAPTER THIRTEEN

Drake opened the front door to Aliandra's cottage and barely had time to catch the large bundle of coat and boy flying through the doorway. All the heat fled from his body as the cold nylon of Tom's jacket hit his bare skin, but the boy's voice full of joy and relief warmed him from the inside.

"You're okay! You're okay." Tom held on as if letting go meant Drake would disappear.

"I'm indeed okay. Thanks to you." Drake squeezed the boy as he knelt to be eye to eye with him. "I understand you were the one who told Aliandra I was in trouble."

Tom nodded so hard his hat fell off. "I saw Viggo take you out of the library."

"You saved me, Tom. You made sure help got to me in time. Well done and thank you." He hugged the boy again.

"I didn't want him to hurt any more people. He wasn't a nice person."

"No, he definitely wasn't that. You did a great job, Tom."

"Are you going to stay with Mama?"

Drake blinked. "Mama?" He shot a look at Aliandra, who smiled and nodded. "Is that what you're calling

145

Aliandra?"

Tom nodded. "She said I could, but I had to ask you if it would be okay to call you Papa Drake. So if you're going to stay, are you going to marry Mama?"

Drake gave Tom his best compassionate smile. "You may call me Papa Drake if you'd like, Tom, but the other question is something I'll have to discuss with Aliandra. But rest your mind at ease, I will definitely be around a lot so you won't have to worry."

"Why can't you tell me?" Tom's lower lip puffed out and Drake swallowed a grin.

"Because it's not up to you. This decision is all hers." Drake patted his shoulder. "Something you should learn right now. If you're ever interested in females of any species, the choice is ultimately theirs. So I can't give you an answer until I discuss it with her."

Tom opened his mouth to protest, but closed it when he looked at Aliandra. Drake's mate hadn't said a word, but the raised eyebrows spoke volumes.

"Okay, Papa Drake."

"Good man. Now, how about we get you to bed? I'll even tell you a bedtime story."

"But I'm not even..." Tom's jaw popped as he yawned widely. "Tired."

"No, of course not. That's why I'll tell you a story while you get ready for bed."

"Okay." Tom shrugged out of his jacket and Aliandra took it while Drake ushered the tired dragonet into the bedroom he'd prepared. "Are you going to stay the night tonight, Drake?"

Drake smiled and nodded. "Going to have to. It's too cold outside to go out in just a towel and my clothes are ruined."

Tom pulled off his shoes and pants, and crawled under the bedcovers Drake held open. "Did Viggo hurt you bad?"

Drake sighed as he sat down on the bed, trying to find

the best way to answer. "He did, Tom. He was a very bad man. I think he would qualify as insane."

"But you're okay now, right?"

"I am, thank you." Drake gave Tom a one-armed hug. "It's because of you and Aliandra that I'm safe and sound. I'll always be grateful for your help."

"You're welcome." Tom settled back into the pillows. "I like it here. It smells good."

"Yes, I agree. So." Drake cleared his throat. "What kind of bedtime story would you like?"

****

Aliandra listened to Drake telling Tom a bedtime story with half an ear as she undressed in her bedroom. She'd found Drake's ruined clothing in the bathtub. The shirt was beyond saving, but she soaked his pants in warm water mixed liberally with white vinegar in hopes it would take the blood stains out.

She rubbed her face as she slipped a silk nightie and matching robe over her shoulders. Normally she wore nothing to bed, but she had a son now and she'd have to determine some new parameters when it came to how she behaved at home. While normal dragons didn't have problems with nudity, Tom had been with Dr. Lance for a long time and Goddess knew Lance had been severely uptight. She swallowed a growl at the thought of the Sword of God so close to Tomarrion.

I bet the bloody bastard had a hand in killing Tom's family.

She wished she could kill Lance all over again, but instead she closed her eyes and breathed deeply before she set fire to her bedroom. *Drake and Tom are safe, and here, and mine.* The Sword of God fanatic existed as nothing more than a disturbing memory, and the Elder Races were safe once more.

For how long?

Only the Goddess knew the answer to such questions and She wasn't talking. Aliandra let her anger flow out with her breath. It took her several breaths to get rid of it all, but by the time Drake wrapped his arms around her waist from behind, she'd relaxed enough not to torch the place.

"You're beautiful." Drake's whispered words warmed her in a completely different way.

"Thank you, *sa kierna*. I think the same of you." She turned in his arms, staring up into his chocolate brown eyes. "Is Tom asleep?"

"Yes. Out cold. I think he was exhausted from more than just today's events."

"It has been a rough few weeks." Aliandra nodded, hoping the dragonet would get plenty of rest. "What story did you tell him?"

Drake gave her a smug smile. "The Dragon and the Prince."

"Oh, is this a relatively new story?" She matched his smile.

"Oh no, this one has ancient beginnings, something like six hundred years ago." He tightened his grip on her waist, hauling her close to his chest. "It started when the Prince's father taught him to honor dragons above all, even if neither of them had ever seen a real dragon."

Aliandra tilted her head. "No? When was the first time for you?"

"The Great Chicago Fire." When Aliandra raised her eyebrows, he nodded. "I happened to be in town visiting the University of Chicago when the fight between a dragon and a demon broke out. I wasn't the only one to see the dragon, but everyone else rationalized it away or they were thrown into sanatoriums. That's when I knew you were real."

"I know that story. A great dragon warrior almost died

in that battle. I hear his family lives in upstate New York now." Aliandra waved it away. "But how did you finish the story to Tom?"

"Oh, the story's not finished." Drake grinned. "The best stories never are."

"Oh, no? How would you continue the story?"

Drake slid his hands into her hair and loosened the braid, pulling the hair forward so he could inhale its scent. He smiled before he tilted his head and kissed her neck below her ear, holding her tightly against his chest. His cock pressed against her belly through the towel and the sensation of his hard body only added to the arousal generated by his kisses.

"Oh, Goddess, Drake. I give you all week to stop doing that."

His deep chuckle rumbled through her as he laid more tickling kisses on her neck. "I think that's a start."

"But we should probably shut the door in case Tom wakes and comes looking for us."

He groaned as he released her, but it was good-natured. "I'll close the door."

She laughed as he reluctantly walked away from her, admiring his backside wrapped in the tight towel. "I was surprised to see you still in the towel when we got home."

"I didn't have any other clothes to wear and I wasn't going out in the snow like this." He shrugged as he returned to her beside the bed. "The towel works for now."

Aliandra's lips curled into a sultry smirk. "If I had my way, you wouldn't even need the towel while at home." She tucked her fingers in between the terry cloth and his hip and tugged. "Don't worry, *sa kierna*, I promise to keep you warm enough to go without."

He grinned and let her take the towel, his cock springing free. Before she could run her hands over it, he pressed his groin against her belly again and tightened his arms around her. "I'll hold you to that, sweetheart. But right now you're wearing entirely too much clothing."

"A robe and a nightie are too much clothing?"

"For what I have in mind, yes."

He peeled the robe off her shoulders and followed silk with soft kisses electrifying her core. She sighed, ending in a whimper when he pulled the strap if her nightie down and kissed her exposed breast.

"I'm going to feast on these tonight, Aliandra. I've been dreaming about them since the night we had dinner."

"Then I'd say you're overdue." She arched her back and pressed her nipple into his mouth. His hard canines slid over the taut skin and sent a shiver straight to her pussy. "Oh, yes, right there, Drake."

He rumbled a chuckle around her breast as he suckled on the nipple, making short work of the other strap of her nightie with his free hand. He cupped her flesh, stroking the other nipple with his thumb until it hardened with desire.

Aliandra moaned and wiggled her hips, reveling in the hard shaft pressed against her mound. "Oh, Drake, stop teasing me and let me do something about this stiff cock of yours."

"Such language from a lady." He rubbed his cock against her harder and shot her a grin.

"I'm not a lady, I'm a dragon and I always get what I want." She snaked her hand between their bodies and stroked his rigid flesh with insistent fingers.

Drake gasped and his eyes flared with arousal. "Oh, I'm going to give you what you want, sweetheart, but it'll be on my terms. I am the notorious Vlad Drakul, the Dragon Prince, and I vow to honor the Order of the Dragon as charged by my father."

"How do you propose to do that, Dragon Prince?" Aliandra teased him by squeezing his cock harder.

"Ooohhh." Drake took a moment to gather his breath before he gently disengaged her hand from his shaft and shoved her nightie down off her hips. "By giving my dragon lady as much pleasure as she can stand tonight before pledging to be hers for all time."

He urged her back onto the bed and spread her legs as he dropped to his knees between them. He licked his lips as he ran his hand over her belly and mound, his thumbs gently parting her nether lips to expose her clit. The scent of her arousal reached her nose just as the exquisite sensation of a rough callus over her clit zinged through her.

Aliandra arched her back and mewled with delight as he added the slick heat of his tongue to his fingers. The sensation combined with the smooth hardness of his canines on her labia ratcheted up her pleasure. Her pussy spasmed and Drake moaned with the flood of her juices into his mouth. The moan ricocheted through her, making her whimper.

"Oh, Goddess, Drake. I've wanted your tongue and teeth on me. Sweet glory, lick my pussy."

Drake growled in approval, sliding one hand down to her slit while his tongue worked her clit. When she arched her hips up to his mouth, he pushed one finger into her clenching pussy, dragging the pad of his finger along her walls. Aliandra groaned at the erotic intrusion and rocked her hips against him.

He slowly withdrew his finger as he lapped at her labia, alternating attention on her lips and clit. When he added a second finger, Aliandra keened her pleasure, clamping down on his digits as he hummed against her sensitive flesh. She rocked her hips on his thrusting fingers, jumping higher and higher in her arousal with each swipe of his tongue on her clit.

When Drake curled his fingers to rub them across her most sensitive spot, Aliandra's orgasm hit her before she even sensed its arrival. She lost her ability to breathe along with her voice as she shot out among the stars of pleasure. Her ecstasy blazed a trail brighter than a comet's tail as she sailed to greater heights.

Drake pumped his hand, milking her as he moaned and slurped up her release, his pleasure and satisfaction as arousing as the efforts he made to bring it to her. At last, she floated down from her high and slowly relaxed her legs from their crushing grip on his shoulders. *Great Fire, I'll have to be more careful next time.* She hadn't considered her strength when she tipped over the edge of orgasm.

"Oh, you are so beautiful when you come, Aliandra." Drake licked his lips as he unhooked her legs from his shoulders.

She snorted, but couldn't help her smile. "I've heard that before, but what's so pretty about it? Most people look like they're in extreme pain when they orgasm."

"Perhaps." Drake crawled up onto the bed and gathered her into his arms, his cock pressed against her side. "But I know you're reveling in pleasure and joy. I can feel it, and that makes it both beautiful and satisfying for me. I take great pride in bringing you pleasure."

His response warmed her from the inside out, but the presence of his hot and hard cock nudging her hip reminded her she had some more pleasurable work to do.

"I'm glad we're in agreement on that." She rolled over on top of him, trapping his swollen shaft between them as she pressed her breasts against his lightly furred chest. The soft hairs tickled her nipples and added another level of pleasure to the hardness against her clit. "Oh, Drake, your cock feels lovely and I need more of you. In fact, I need you every day, every night, for as long as dragonly possible."

"Dragonly possible?" He raised an eyebrow in amusement as he rolled his hips against her, setting off sparks behind her eyes. "I'm not familiar with that phrase."

"You're a knight in the Order of the Dragon, correct?"

"Yes." He smirked as he rolled his hips again, grinding his lovely, hard flesh on her pussy.

"And you're the True Mate to a dragon, now, so…"

"Wait, what?" He stopped and met her gaze, his chocolate eyes open wide. "I'm what now?"

"The True Mate to a dragon. My True Mate." She stopped moving and stared at him, her gut sinking in trepidation. *Hellwinds, is he going to run again?* "We true mated the night you came with the roses. You honestly didn't know?"

Sorrow swelled in her chest as the silence stretched and she tried to hold it at bay, but it seeped into the crevices of her heart and spread blackness in her soul. If he ran now, she didn't know if she'd ever recover.

CHAPTER FOURTEEN

Drake blinked. *I true mated her that night?* Amazement cut off his breath and his voice. *How the hell did I true mate her and not know it?* There'd been very few times he'd been so blind to things, but this had to be the worst moment ever. *I'm a damn fool.*

But he realized some part of him knew, the same part urging him to see her despite his mind telling him to stay away. The same part of him turning its nose up at the blood of anyone other than Aliandra. If he'd true mated her, he wouldn't be interested in feeding from any other being. *Hell, I can't feed from anything else and be satisfied. Like eating Chinese food full of MSG.*

"Drake?" Aliandra's expression turned sad and she shifted to move off of him, but he caught her hips and held her still.

"I'm sorry, I'm still processing."

Aliandra nodded, her lids dropping over her glorious eyes. "Right. I didn't realize you didn't know, but that explains a lot. Let me see if I can find some clothes for you so you can go home."

"No. Wait. Please, Aliandra. Give me a moment to understand my great good fortune."

"What?" Her gaze sharpened and some of the animation returned to her face.

Drake gave her a grimace. "I've been such an unmitigated jackass and so caught up in what I perceived as being dishonorable, I failed to notice when I'd gotten exactly what I dreamed of having."

She narrowed her eyes, but said nothing, waiting for him to explain. He chose his words carefully to be as clear as possible.

"It should've been clear from the way your blood affected me and from the lack of hunger cravings after I fed on you that I'd found my mate, but I didn't pay attention to the signs." He sighed, but kept his grip on her hips. She was stronger than him, but he'd do his best to keep her on top of him. "Some part of me knew we'd made a connection, but I couldn't get past what my mind said was happening. Please forgive me, Aliandra. I was so blinded by the past, I couldn't see the present. I couldn't see what you'd given me."

She bit her lip and frowned. "You're not apologizing, are you?"

"Only for being too stupid to see what was right in front of me. But not for being with you or for true mating you that night. For that, I'll be forever grateful." He squeezed her hips with his hands. "Please, Aliandra. Forgive me for being a daft, self-absorbed fool, and let me make it up to you tonight. Let me love you the way I've dreamed without the constraints of the 'should-bes.'"

She tilted her head, but her frown lines smoothed. "And how would you do that?"

"Ride me, dragon lady. Ride me hard until you can't hold back. Take my cock and use it for your pleasure." Said piece of anatomy already grew to uphold its promise. "I'm here to serve you as my lady and my lover. You're the one who makes my existence extraordinary and I will honor you with whatever service I can provide. You are the dragon I'm meant to serve, not an old knightly order or a forgotten ruler. It's you, Aliandra. It always has been you. It's just taken until now for me to see it."

She bit her bottom lip as she considered.

"I'll make you a deal, Drake. I'll let you serve me and honor me if you truly become my mate and my husband, and help me raise that lovely dragonet in there." Aliandra pointed to the hallway where Tom slept in the room beyond. "What do you say?"

Drake didn't think he could have found a better solution to the prophecy or his desires. That Aliandra wanted him and wanted his companionship in being parents to an orphaned dragon warmed him more than Iris's Irish Cream coffee at the café.

"I say you've got yourself a deal, sweetheart."

"Good. Now fuck me hard because I want to be tired and well satisfied, and I've heard vampires have great stamina." Aliandra gave him a challenging smirk.

"And where have you heard this?" Drake raised an eyebrow as he thumbed her nipples into hard peaks.

"I have my sources, but I prefer to do my own research."

He laughed as her eyes flared with arousal. "I think you should put your knowledge to the test. Find out if I live up to rumor." He licked his lips and she grinned. "I only have one requirement before we start."

"And what's that?" She wriggled on top of him and his cock stiffened.

"That you come with me, that you take your pleasure with me so I can see and feel it along with mine. As your knight, it's my duty to see to your pleasure, and in turn, that brings me greater satisfaction."

"You drive a hard deal, Drake MacGregor, but I accept. Let's see you put your cock where your mouth was."

Aliandra grasped his hard shaft and positioned the

head at her entrance, grinning so wide her elongated canines showed between her lips. He held her hips as she slowly, torturously sank down on his cock. Drake moaned as slick, wet heat engulfed his flesh and pleasure shot up his spine.

"Oh, sweet Goddess, Aliandra. You take my breath away."

"All evidence to the contrary," she quipped, but her expression showed her own pleasure. "But I shall do my best."

She paused when he was seated balls-deep in her pussy and opened her peacock-green eyes. So many emotions roiled there; love, arousal, pleasure, excitement, and desire. All of them directed at and inspired by him. Awe bloomed in his chest right along with ecstasy. This lovely dragon, a creature beyond his wildest dreams, wanted him and him alone. He would do everything in his power to keep her regard.

Then she squeezed her inner muscles around his cock and his lust took over. Drake arched his hips and pulled out before slamming back into her. She moaned with pleasure and rocked her own hips harder. She tightened her grip on his shoulders as she braced her weight on her hands, lifting off him to ride.

"You're mine, Aliandra, my dragon lady. Take your pleasure from me." His growl sounded more like a crazed beast than a refined, educated man, but he didn't care. He wanted her and wanted to give her such pleasure she'd never forget his love for her.

Their matched thrusts increased in frequency and his release boiled in his balls as she rode him as hard as he could wish. Her breasts bounced on her chest and he grasped them, thumbing the nipples as she threw her head back.

"Oh, Goddess, Drake. I'm going to come!"

Drake snarled and thrust harder, grabbing her hips to

get the best leverage. Aliandra tightened on his cock and keened her pleasure as she tipped over the edge of orgasm. Her pleasure sparked his and he tumbled after her, his release boiling out of his balls and filling her with his seed.

She continued to rock on him, milking his cock and whimpering her ecstatic release. He tried to focus on her expression, but his own pleasure had him sitting up and sinking his fangs into her neck. He could no more stop himself from feeding off her than he could stop the snow flurrying outside.

Aliandra shrieked and tightened on his cock again as he dragged several swallows of her blood into his mouth. Sweet coppery bliss filled his taste buds and sent his mind reeling with pleasure. He swallowed, pulled his teeth out of her, and licked the wound to seal it.

She sighed before she bent and sank her own canines into his shoulder. The initial pain gave way to exquisite pleasure and shot him into the stars for another orgasm. His cock flexed in her pussy and his balls tightened up against his base while he shuddered in ecstasy.

At last they both came down from their atmospheric highs and she released his shoulder, licking the puncture with her tongue. Pleasure ricocheted through him at the hot, slick touch, but his body only shivered, too tired to do anything else. She gently rolled off him and snuggled against his side, wrapping her arm around his belly.

"You're mine and I'm keeping you, *sa kierna*." The satisfaction in her voice filled his soul with contentment.

"So glad you noticed." A contented smile stretched his lips. "I hope you'll continue to notice for the rest of our lives together."

"Oh, I will. Just remember I will hoard our moments together like precious jewels. It's what dragons do."

"I shall remember." He kissed her soundly, licking her long canines and making her tremble. "By order of the dragon, I shall remember."

"No, doctor's orders. Your health is my primary concern." Aliandra winked. "In fact, I think you need more sexual exercise. You haven't had nearly enough." She pulled him on top of her and licked his throat beside his ear.

Drake groaned as his cock stiffened. "As my dragon lady commands."

"Damn right." She grinned. "I love you, Drake."

"I love you, Aliandra." And he slid his cock home.

THE END

A WALK IN THE SAND
THE IVORY ROAD, BOOK 1
SNEEK PEEK

The adventure of Ivory's lifetime might just be the death of her...

When it comes to make believe, A-list actress Ivory is a professional. But when a desert hike takes her across a dimensional rift, her real-life self, Iliana Rory, must separate fantasy from reality. The man she swears is the costar in her next movie might share the same surname and appearance, but there are no sets in this Mr. Crowe's world, no props, and no director to yell "cut" before blood is spilled.

With a fortune in stolen treasure and the forces of the Knalish army hot on their trail, Brandon Crowe and his partner, Ahmad, must cross a desert neither of them knows well. Mistaken for their guide, Iliana seizes any chance to stay ahead of the army and survive in this new world.

Adventure straight out of a Hollywood blockbuster might be on Iliana's bucket-list, but she never dreamed there'd be the real possibility of death when the end credits roll. A Walk in the Sand is the first story in the four part serial recounting Iliana's journey along the Ivory Road.

THE NAVY'S GHOST
BAD BOYS OF BETA SQUAD, BOOK 1
SNEEK PEEK

A SEAL is strongest with her Team…

Ensign Christiana "Ghost" Brickman is the only female SEAL to survive BUD/S training, a real Navy Jane. But when an ambush ends her career as an active SEAL, she's free to pursue other interests. Like her two best friends Lt. Jim "Retro" Waters and Chief Warrant Officer Todd "Magic" Hunter. She's wanted them for over a year, but never dared to approach them while in the squad.

Retro has fought his dark desires since high school, certain the need to share a woman unnatural. Magic had never considered sharing before Ghost mentions it, but it solves his dilemma of choosing between his best friend and his woman. But Retro balks at Ghost's offer to share and retreats from both when she marries Magic.

Everyone feels Retro's loss, but he ignores the ache of their broken connection in favor of living 'normal.' When Ghost and the other wives of Beta Squad are kidnapped, Retro must reevaluate how much both Ghost and Magic mean to him. And he must decide how far he's willing to go to save the woman he loves, before she becomes the Navy's ghost.

OTHER BOOKS BY SIOBHAN MUIR

Her Devoted Vampire (from Evernight Publishing)
Queen Bitch of the Callowwood Pack (from Siren Publishing)
Not a Dragon's Standard Virgin (from Siren Publishing)

Cloudburst Colorado Series
A Hell Hound's Fire (from Three Lakes Books)
The Beltane Witch (from Three Lakes Books)

Christmas I.C.E. Magic (Happy Holidays from the Crescent Moon Lodge Anthology)
Cloudburst Ice Magic (from Three Lakes Books)

Rifts Series
Take the Reins (from Three Lakes Books)
A Centaur's Solstice Wish (from Three Lakes Books)

Bad Boys of Beta Squad Series
Bronco's Rough Ride (from Three Lakes Books)
The Navy's Ghost (from Three Lakes Books)

The Ivory Road
A Walk in the Sand (from Three Lakes Books)
Outback Dreams (from Three Lakes Books)

Coming Soon
Rimshot's Hard Target (Bad Boys of Beta Squad #3)
Second Chance Succubus
Cloudburst Coffee & Spa (Cloudburst Colorado #4)

ABOUT THE AUTHOR

Siobhan Muir lives in Cheyenne, Wyoming, with her husband, two daughters, and a vegetarian cat she swears is a shape-shifter, though he's never shifted when she can see him. When not writing, she can be found looking down a microscope at fossil fox teeth, pursuing her other love, paleontology. An avid reader of science fiction/fantasy, her husband gave her a paranormal romance for Christmas one year, and she was hooked for good.

In previous lives, Siobhan has been an actor at the Colorado Renaissance Festival, a field geologist in the Aleutian Islands, and restored inter-planetary imagery at the USGS. She's hiked to the top of Mount St. Helens and to the bottom of Meteor Crater.

Siobhan writes kick-ass adventure with hot sex for men and women to enjoy. She believes in happily ever after, redemption, and communication, all of which you will find in her paranormal romance stories.

Connect with Siobhan online at:
http://siobhanmuir.com
http://www.facebook.com/siobhan.muir.35
http://www.tsu.co/SiobhanMuir
http://twitter.com/SiobhanMuir
http://siobhanmuir.blogspot.com
http://pinterest.com/siobhanmuir.35

www.ingramcontent.com/pod-product-compliance
Lightning Source LLC
Chambersburg PA
CBHW070551180626
46817CB00005B/1782

* 9 780692 497715 *